Herman Charles Merivale, Edgar Giberne

Binko's blues : a Tale for children of all Growths

Herman Charles Merivale, Edgar Giberne

Binko's blues : a Tale for children of all Growths

ISBN/EAN: 9783337024703

Printed in Europe, USA, Canada, Australia, Japan

Cover: Foto ©Andreas Hilbeck / pixelio.de

More available books at **www.hansebooks.com**

BINKO'S BLUES

A Tale for Children of all Growths

HERMAN CHARLES MERIVALE

AUTHOR OF

"FAUCIT OF BALLIOL," "WHITE PILGRIM," ETC.

ILLUSTRATED BY EDGAR GIBERNE

LONDON : CHAPMAN AND HALL

LIMITED

1884

All Dramatic and other Rights Reserved.

TO

MY LITTLE GODCHILD,

Florence Merivale Besley,

AGED THREE AND A HALF.

VIEWFIELD, KENLEY, DECEMBER, 1883.

Tossing in broken slumber to and fro,

By too much journal=reading half distraught,

The latest miracles of modern thought

To living form I saw before me grow!

They came,—the monsters of advertisement,--

From subterranean railways gambolling;

Or springing like weird mushrooms in a night,

On track of fire or house=demolishing,

O'er giant=hoardings in a grisly row;

Heads one half chestnut=brown, the other white,

Strange drinks red=lettered over gaudy bars,

Wild phantom ships and ghastly pickle=jars;

Till as I wondered why such dreams were sent,

A voice said, "We are fairies: rise and write."

CONTENTS.

CHAPTER VIII.

CHAPTER IX.

CHAPTER X.

CHAPTER XI.

CHAPTER XII.

CHAPTER XIII.

CHAPTER XIV.

CHAPTER XV.

BINKO'S BLUES:

A TALE FOR CHILDREN OF ALL GROWTHS.

CHAPTER I.

A HISTORICAL SKETCH OF TADT.

THERE was great excitement in the kingdom of Tadt. It was an exceedingly old and venerable kingdom, and the sceptre had been handed down with great regularity from father to son, for nobody quite knows how many billion years. For a long time Tadt had been supposed, as a kingdom, to be nearly as old as the creation. But a committee of Tadtite sages, who had appointed themselves a committee because they had nothing better to do, had succeeded in proving to their own satisfaction

h,

B

and the puzzling of everybody else, that the first
Tadtites must have been made several ages before
there was any creation, and first saw the light,
(or what there was of it,) at the bottom of the
dirty old pond which had certainly existed in the
market place of the oldest village in the kingdom,

SOME MEMBERS OF THE SAGE-GREEN COMMITTEE.

as long as anything could possibly have existed
anywhere. The Hair-Professor Shpex, from the
neighbouring empire of Karamsin, having first connected Karamsin and Tadt (which, as you all must
know, is an island) by a submarine steam balloon,
impelled by electric eels, (with the help of the

draught which made the bottom of the water so cold,) had established to the full conviction of the Sage-green Committee, as it was called, of which he was a corresponding member, that the first Tadtite king was also the first oyster, and proceeded, at an hour some day to be settled, in an imperfect condition of legs and arms, from the chick of the original Tadt-Pole, which stood upright on its tail at the bottom of the pond. Whether the chick or the pole was itself alive at the time, and if not, how the oyster became so, also how the pole got there, or indeed what There exactly was, Shpex left with confidence to the next generation. Every succeeding generation, as he showed, would, by perseverance on the part of the Sage-green Committee, (to be re-appointed by itself from time to time, with full powers to be cock-sure about everything,) push the first question a billion or two of years farther back, until the whole thing came to an end, and met the other end somewhere else, and then it would all begin again. The square, being then complete, would have nothing to do but go round in a circle, and the entire simplicity of everything would be plain to everybody. Shpex saw it all, all the time, but his countrymen, thanks partly to a habit of putting all their verbs in the wrong places, had a difficulty of expressing their thoughts as clearly. as they always said they thought them, and Shpex, though a Hair-Professor, (called so because he so seldom cut it,) was not an exception, and the masses could not understand him. It was stupid of the masses; but they made a foolishly large proportion of the people of Tadt; and till they quite understood and believed all he meant, (or at all events believed it; the understanding might come afterwards,) Shpex's mission would have been only partly successful. The trying part of the whole thing was clearly this : that nothing ever exactly began, or could ever exactly end, exactly anywhere. Shpex himself once admitted, that what there was outside Space rather puzzled him; also what there was inside Space before there was any

Space. Shpex, after the manner of his nation, began to ask himself these riddles when he was a very small boy; and then when he went to sleep he used sometimes to dream of building a very high wall all round Space, which nobody should go beyond. But just when it was finished he used to dream of tumbling right over on the other side, and never getting to any bottom of anything. For there certainly were difficulties connected with the general size of everything which nothing seemed to get over; and why shouldn't anybody go anywhere, where there cannot be anywhere where anything can stop? Even conundrums like Shpex's can't stop. The sound of a bad riddle, once asked, is eternally going on somewhere or somewhere else, without any answer, unless it is given at once. And then the answer goes on too. It is awful to think about; and ought to prevent anybody from ever asking a riddle.

Now the point of all this (and there is a point in everything if you only know where to look

for it) is, that I cannot tell you the latitude and
longitude of Tadt, because it is outside the Map.
When you come to think of it, you will see that
there must be a great many places that are. (I
will tell you at once that Tadt is pronounced Tad
in Tadt, and Tart in Karamsin, where they spell
and pronounce everything in a very odd way.)
A Tadtite boy, being asked at school not long
ago what was "the latitude," answered that "it
was a line which ran all over the map, crossing
mountains and rivers in its course, and then
empties itself into the longitude." He must have
meant the other map, of course, because there
must be maps of some kind in Tadt, or else there
could be no schools. And then there would be
no School-Benches, and the government couldn't go
on. That is all I know about the latitude and
longitude of Tadt. It is somewhere; so there is
plenty of room for it.

There was great excitement in the kingdom of
Tadt. For there had been kings in Tadt ever since
the time of that first oyster, as to whom Shpex

had not decided whether he was originally a native, or a settler. King Hoppo the First had succeeded to King Echo the First, and King Echo the Second to King Hoppo the First; and so on through a series of Echoes and Hoppoes quite innumerable, till the history of Tadt was written in such an astonishing number of volumes, that parents, and guardians, and teachers were fairly puzzled what to do with it, and at last hit upon the idea of beginning at the other end, and teaching history backwards from the present day, so that a pupil might go back as far as he could before he died. The first thing the pupils had to do after they had learned how to read, was to go through the summary of events in the *True Tadtite* every morning, and then refer to the Home News and the Foreign Correspondence to find out how far it was true. And long before they had quite done that, lessons were generally over for the day. Besides that, they had to find out the meaning of all the foreign words whenever they met them, and look out all the places

mentioned in the map (the other map, you know)
as they came. So the little Tadtites learned
history, and languages, and geography backwards
all at once. Though, indeed, as to languages, the
greatest difficulty they had in reading the *True
Tadtite*, very often was how to learn their own.
The President of the first Tadtite School-Bench
had carried this.system of education against great
opposition, when it began to be found out that, in
consequence of the great number of old kings who
had left nothing remarkable behind them except
their dates, the old kind of lessons were becoming
quite impossible ; and all the little boys and girls—
the girls particularly—were beginning to think of
nothing except the secret of the original Tadt-Pole,
to talk of nothing except their own descent from
it, and generally to become such tremendous little
prigs that there was no putting up with them.
So when things grew so bad that they couldn't
grow worse, the President introduced this new
style of teaching, and everything became comfort-
able again. The young Tadtites again enjoyed

what they were taught, and grew up happy and useful little Tadtites, instead of being very sad, and of no use at all to anybody. The Sage-green Committee were very much disgusted with the President of the School-Bench, and proved in the most positive manner that he was ruining the Mind of the country. The Karamsin newspapers joined them ; and the *All-over-the-place-Universal-Wisdom-and-Strength-Gazette*, which is the nearest translation I can arrive at of the name of the principal one, made some very heavy jokes about him which only a Karamsinian could laugh at. But the President had his way, for all that.

Now such of the little Tadtites as were clever and forward, were allowed to study another part of the *True Tadtite* as well as those which I have pointed out, and to read the reports of the debates which went on in the Chamber of Notables, better known as the Uncommons, or Tadtite Governing Chamber. When they had read the debates through as well as they could, they were expected to bring two abstracts of them to the teacher ;

c

the first containing in the shortest space all that
had anything to do with the subject being debated,
and the second all that could be of any use whatever to the government of the country. The
debates generally filled half the *True Tadtite*
when the Uncommons were sitting; but the boy
who got the first prize at an examination, after
the longest debate of all, brought the first abstract
on one sheet of note-paper, and the second on
a blank page.

It must not be supposed, however, that Tadt
was not well governed; because it was; better
perhaps on the whole than any other country
in the other map. But that was because the
king did not meddle with the Uncommons, but left
it to do, or rather to talk, very much as it liked.
The Uncommons were made up practically of men
of three parties—the Thigs, the Wories, and the
Goroos. The Thigs and the Wories used to get
into power about turn-and-turn about, and had
on the whole very much the same ideas about a
great many things, though they were obliged to

call each -other the most dreadful names in order to keep up the fun, without which it was agreed that the country could not have got on. The government of the island was really carried out by a set of quiet people who worked in their offices and did not go near the Uncommons, and kept on in exactly the same way whether the governing party were Thigs or Wories. They were not paid as much as the gentlemen in the Uncommons who were supposed to manage the offices ; but then their pay lasted a good deal longer. Their chief difficulty, perhaps, was that these supposed managers were changed so often, that the quiet people were obliged to lose a great deal of valuable time in teaching every new man his business. For it was an odd rule that in order to give the members of the Uncommons a good training, the chief chosen for each office was generally the one in the governing body who appeared to the public to know least about it before. However, it all went on very well on the whole, and did not much matter.

I don't want to say much about the Goroos,
because they were rather dreadful people. They
were a knot of men who came from a small colony
of Tadt, where the people were very warm-hearted
and amusing, but very lazy, and wanted to have
enough to live upon without doing any work for
it. So when a famine set in, which of course
couldn't help happening every now and then, as
a natural consequence, they used (being put up
to it by the Goroos) to cut off the tails of their
neighbours' cows to make things better; and
when that plan didn't succeed, to cut the throats
of their neighbours themselves, in order to make
things uncomfortable generally. Of course, the
King of Tadt and the Uncommons couldn't allow
that : so they were obliged to put some of them
in prison, and cut off the heads of some of the
worst. The Goroos, that is the gentlemen from
the colony who came to the Uncommons, used
to make a great many speeches to prove that it
was very wrong of Tadt to treat the colonists in
that way. Which no doubt was true ; because

the heads to be cut off ought of course to have
been their own instead. But that was one of
the many things which ought to be done, but
can't be. For it was a very odd fact that the
gentlemen in the Uncommons, while they were
all dreadfully rude all round in small matters,
were quite as much afraid of telling each other
the truth about big ones, and would have called
a toad or a harrow their "honourable friend"
if it got in among them.

Now I wish you all to understand at once, that
I am not going to give you very much more
of this sort to read, because what I have to tell
you is after all only a fairy-history of the singular adventures that happened to my heroine,
to whom I am going to introduce you in the
course of a chapter or two. But I think that
you would like to know just a little about the
kingdom in which she was born, so that we may
all have a general idea where we are before we
start on our real journey. And as my heroine was
no less a person than the girl-queen of the wonderful

country which I have been talking about, of
course it would be 'very wrong if you did not
learn something of its ways and its constitution.
I have told you that it was an island, sur-
rounded on all its four sides by water! Once
it had only three sides, because a very clever
man, called Sir Aurifame, built a tunnel all the
way under the sea to the pretty country of
Cimarosa, which was Tadt's nearest neighbour,
in order to make everybody friends, and to
bring money and merchandise into the island.
Neither the Thigs nor the Wories liked it; but
he went on about it so long, and gave them
so many luncheons and so much wine to drink,
that at last they all gave in. Well—the tunnel
was made; and then what happened was just
what all sensible people expected. The Tadtites
had been so accustomed to live in a country
where nobody could get at them, that they could
never think of anything except that the Cimarosians or somebody else wanted to invade them
without rhyme or reason. So they went on

having panics; taking all their money out of all the banks, and putting it all in again, till the banks were all ruined; going up in large bodies to Kashburg, which was the name of their capital city; and insisting on having the tunnel blown up, and Sir Aurifame hanged—till nobody could stand it any longer. The Principal Minister of Tadt called a council of Thigs and Wories together, which was quite unanimous. Even the Goroos had no objections to make. The tunnel was blown up in the night and Sir Aurifame banished to a distant island, and everything settled down again. Everybody had to travel by sea as usual till the Hair-Professor invented his balloon for his own use, with which nobody interfered. Now you know all about the history of Tadt, to begin with, that you need know, and I can go on with my story.

CHAPTER II.

THERE was great excitement in the kingdom of Tadt. I have told you that twice before ; but the oftener I tell it, the easier it becomes to remember. That is the great leading principle which the gentlemen in the Uncommons had always to bear in mind when they made their speeches, because if they never said the same thing more than once, hardly· any speech could last more than ten minutes, and hardly anybody could make more than one speech in a month, and that would never have done. And the secret of all the excitement was this : that the beautiful queen of the island, Floriline the Fragrant, was going to be married upon the day on which my true history opens. It is always very delightful when anybody is going to be married, but you cannot often catch a queen for it.

Floriline was the daughter and only child of King Hoppo M., (which, as we all know, means Hoppo the Thousandth,) and there was for a very long time a strong feeling that she had not done her duty to the country by being a girl. Moreover, it was doubtful if she could be a girl, by law. For, as I have already said, the Echoes and the Hoppoes had succeeded each other on the throne of Tadt with absolute regularity ever since there was a Tadt, and there had never been anything but kings in the country before. Many generations back there had appeared to be some danger of there being no male heir to the succession. In that case a very strong-minded maiden-relative of the reigning sovereign, known as Aunt Sally, might, it was feared, legally claim the throne. She was a great champion of women's rights,

D

and took a leading part at all the School-Benches
and skirt-reform meetings. She was not at all
good looking, and had a habit of standing in the
middle of her palace grounds smoking a short
pipe, which bad little boys used to shy sticks at
whenever they got a chance. Now, her nephew,
a King Echo, was dangerously ill, and Aunt Sally
made no secret of all that she intended to do for
her sex when she came to the throne. She had a
great party of sympathisers in the country, who
called themselves the Sentimentals, and had succeeded in sending half a score of members to the
Uncommons, who made quite as much noise there
as if they had been half a thousand. And she had
some strong friends upon the Sage-green Committee
of that day, who liked old women's gossip very
much themselves, and thought that public affairs
would be much better for a strong infusion of it.
So that when a Succession Bill, to settle who was to
reign over the country if the king died without
leaving a son, was introduced into the Uncommons,
there was nearly a revolution over the excitement

it created. But the majority succeeded in winning
the day, and making a law that no woman should
be allowed to reign in Tadt, which was very
properly called the Sallic Law. The throne was to
pass to a cousin of the king's, the head of the
princely house of Binko. The whole history of
Tadt was nearly changed by this. The Aunt Sally
party grew very violent and very strong. The lady
went all round the country and made speeches
which everybody said were quite as good as the
men's, while their language was, if anything, rather
stronger. The Binko party, on their side, took to
carrying revolvers and wearing trousers, (up to that
time, everything being peaceful, men had all dressed
in flowing garments,) and it seemed quite certain
that when the reigning King Echo died, which was
close at hand, there would have to be a fight for it
in spite of the new law. But just when all the
court doctors agreed in print that the king
couldn't live another twenty-four hours, and the
True Tadtite published a leading article with a
black border all about his death and what a good

man he had always been, one of those provoking
things happened which are always so fond of hap‑
pening, especially when people will prophecy about
them before they have happened. A poet once
wrote an ode about a mad dog that bit a man; and
the ode, as many of you know, ends in this way:

> "*The wound it seemed both sore and sad*
> *To every Christian eye:*
> *And while they swore the dog was mad,*
> *They swore the man would die.*
>
> "*But soon a wonder came to light,*
> *That showed the rogues they lied;*
> *The man recovered of the bite,*
> *The dog it was that died.*"

Now that is just what happened here. Aunt Sally,
everybody knew, would live to be a hundred. But
on the very day when the doctors gave King Echo
up, Aunt Sally was resting in her favourite attitude
in her garden after an unusually exhausting speech,
and some naughty boys began to throw sticks at
her. One threw with too good an aim, and broke

her pipe off so short and so near the mouth that he broke her front teeth with it, and caused concussion of the brain, of which she died in the night. And on the very morning when the *True Tadtite* published the article on the king's death and Aunt Sally's prospects, Aunt Sally was dead and the king was recovering. The little boy was soundly flogged first, and had his head cut off afterwards, murmuring with his last breath that the first hurt most. The king got well very fast, and then had a son who was christened Hoppo, and came to the throne in due course of time in the usual way. The Binkoes tried to get up an agitation about his being a stolen child and not a real prince, but they were unanimously set upon and driven out of the country. So everything went on peacefully and regularly as before, and the only danger there had ever been of a civil war in Tadt was quietly Tadted —I mean tided—over.

Once upon a time, then, there was a great fear of things going wrong in Tadt, and of a king leaving no son behind him. But in the instance of the

history which I am writing something quite unusual
happened—quite unusual, at all events, in any well-
regulated fairy history, for the same thing happened
twice upon a time. A great many years—ever so
great many years—after Aunt Sally was gathered
to her mothers, and was only remembered in the
shape of a game invented to celebrate her history
for the amusement of the young school children of
Tadt, and played chiefly on race-courses, King
Hoppo M. died for no particular reason, one hour
after the court doctors had just agreed in print
that he would be quite well enough to hold a Private
Council the next morning. He was young and
only lately married, and he had been dead six
months when his only child was born. Everybody
knew that the child was to be a boy, because the
law had long ago decided that it must. And the
rejoicings were all ready, and the fireworks all
properly primed, and all the bells had ordered new
clappers and had them made, at the time when
everything was waiting for the birth of Echo the
thousand-and-first. But when it happened, he was

born a little girl, which was just like his perversity.
As soon as it became an established fact throughout
the kingdom of Tadt that a little girl he actually
was—which took a long time, because it was illegal
and nobody would believe it—the first danger of a
revolution was past, the heir being by that time
seven years old. The fact of its sex had taken
seven years to establish, because one of the wisest
of the counsellors of the queen-mother, poor Helenamaia, discovered that the thing to be done in order
to save her from being executed or banished for her
contrariness was to gain time, and that the only
way to gain time was to put the question into
chancery. The opinion of the law officers of the
Crown was therefore asked as to the sex of the
child, the Sallic Law being considered. They agreed
upon the point, and so did all the other Wory
lawyers, that being the party then in power. But the
question was so important that it was submitted to
a committee of the Uncommons, when it was found
that all the Thig lawyers were unanimously of the
opposite opinion. And so they kept the ball going

for seven years until the costs became tremendous. But that did not really matter, because whichever way it went in the end the Crown must win, because whatever won would be the Crown. And the Crown being the people, the people would have to pay the expenses.

When the chiefest and wisest of all the judges of Tadt, the Lord Honidhu, finally came to review the whole matter in the Upper Court, it proved to be so clear and simple that, if it could only have come before him at first, (and he was bound to settle it in the end,) the saving of time and of money would have been wonderful, besides the unimportant addition of the anxiety of the people whose interests were concerned. But there was a great and influential body of men in Tadt called the Rab,* who lived by arguing questions, and would all have to turn their hands to something

---

* The Tadtite language has been sparingly used in this narrative, because it is a history and not a grammar. It is of simple construction, and will be translated with very little trouble. Tadtite words are intimated by asterisks.

else unless every question was fought out in three courts at least, and very often twice in each, besides an intermediate argument each time as to whether it ought to be fought out again or not, which was itself nearly as long a fight as any of the others. And the Rab having long ago settled that the country couldn't go on without them— which the country had accepted as a fact in the stolid and patient sort of way which was characteristic of the people of Tadt—they were not likely to allow a leading case of such importance as this to be decided in a hurry. It was their privilege. And there was nothing in Tadt like a privilege, which was a bore for those who had none. A great many points arose in the course of the case, of which the knotty point was, as the most eloquent member of the Rab put it in a poetical form, (he never spoke for less than a week about anything, and his clients paid him fresh every day,)

"A boy, or not a boy—that is the question."

It sounded simple; but was it a point of fact,

E

or a point of law? The question of fact was of
course straightforward, and decided at once by
the first jury who heard it, and said the child was
a girl at the very first opportunity given them,
which they did not get for some time. But
under the Sallic Act the child had no business to
be a girl, and that was the point of law which
had to be reserved so often that in seven years
it quite spoiled by keeping, and when at the end
of that time the Lord Honidhu finally decided
that it really was a question of fact after all, and
that the decision of the original jury upon a
matter which upon the whole they could decide
as well as anybody else, ought to have been left
alone, a great many people said that for a chief
judge he had not half the respect for the law that
he ought to have. If there hadn't been a real
point of law, how could the thing have lasted so
long? However the Rab had got a good deal
out of it, and felt that at last they could not get
any more.

So the pretty little Floriline grew up to the

age of seven under the care of her mother
Helenamaia, and the kingdom of Tadt was governed
by a regency. There was a good deal of opposition
to the idea though; and for the first time for
a great many generations there was talk abroad
of the claims of the great family of Binko, which
was to have succeeded to the throne under the
Sallic Law, and under the same law claimed now
to be entitled. But the Binko family had not
been doing well in the world. Instead of settling
down like respectable exiles, (they had been
banished from Tadt as I told you,) and giving no
trouble to honest people, they had grown worse
and worse and more restless as time went on,
were always fitting out buccaneering expeditions,
(they were immensely rich,) and issuing the most
shocking proclamations about their rights to the
crown of Tadt, which they claimed to have
properly passed to them under the Sallic Law,
in spite of the subsequent birth of the young
Hoppo who had stepped into their shoes. During
the time of Sir Aurifame's tunnel they threatened

the coasts of Tadt more than ever, and it was
blown up and flooded six times in one year,
because of the state of mind they kept the
Tadtites in. The Thigs and the Wories had a
great time over the bills that the country had
to pay for all this, abused each other dreadfully
for what was no fault of either, and went into
office and out of it like rabbits in a warren. It
was this that at last ended in the final destruction
of the tunnel.

During the seven years while the sex of
Princess Floriline the Fragrant was before the
Courts of Law, it is needless to say that the
excitement among the Binko party was intense,
for there could be no question now that, in spite
of the great popularity of the reigning family
with all classes in the country, and the hatred
and fear in which the name of Binko was held
by all but the dangerous classes, who were not
very dangerous in Tadt, their claim to the crown
under the law which had been passed so long ago
was very formidable indeed. It was true that

it was very long ago; that the times had entirely changed; and that the Princess Floriline was not at all likely to grow up in any likeness to her ancestor Aunt Sally, and showed no disposition in her childhood either for making speeches or for smoking pipes. But there was the law; there was no mistake about it, and law was supreme in Tadt. Indeed if the Tadtites had not been so law-abiding, is it likely that the country could have gone quietly on in its usual way for seven whole years without a revolution, unless it had been felt by all parties that a revolution would never do which was subject to a point of law? The Binko of the day, however, was not idle all this time. He was a terrible Binko indeed. He was short of stature and round of form, and a sinister smile hovered perpetually at the left end of his mouth. His voice was a deep and overpowering bass, changing suddenly sometimes, when he got more excited than usual, into a high shrill scream, and then going back again, till it sounded as if he were

singing duets with himself. At these moments
he would foam ferociously at the right end of
his mouth, while smiling still with the other.
His temper was, in fact, awful. His perpetual
explosions of anger had flown to his head, and
settled in his complexion, particularly round the
nose, where the rich and mottled colours were
aggravated by deep draughts of Nig,* a fiery
spirit which, out of tumblers, was the favourite
drink of Binko. His hair was short and wiry and
of a grizzled black, and stood up close all round
his head without a parting, a fashion which he had
learned when an exile in Cimarosa. He said it
kept his head cool, though it did not appear to do
so. His eyebrows were very shaggy and as white as
anything could be ; his moustache was very long and
thick, and still whiter. The contrast with his nose
was very remarkable ; so much so that just that
section of him and no more had once been painted
and exhibited by a very strange artist at the
Ymedaca,* or great Painter show, in Kashburg,
under the title of "A Lunacy in Red and White.'

He was, to speak plainly, a pirate and a bad one.
He did not care what he pirated; and he drove a
great trade, among many other trades, in abduct-
ing the early manuscripts of Tadtite romances or
Cimarosian plays from their unsuspecting authors,
and exacting a large commission for them in the
distant country with which he chiefly dealt, the
Great Settlements of Dollarosa.   "Anon he would
return"—as the simple chronicles of his race,
which I have obtained from his descendants the
permission to consult, in their own way express
it—"laden with a cargo of very precious explosives
and dangerous substances, manufactured in the
Great Settlements with a view to the destruction
of the buildings, and likewise of the women and
children in Tadt, for the behoof of the Goroo
party who did desire the general unsettlement
and distraction of all things in that country, and
especially of such as could not defend themselves.
True it was that Dollarosa did proclaim that she
regarded Tadt as a friendly country, and could
at any time without difficulty have forbidden

the manufacture and export of the aforesaid
explosive substances, whereof she was studious to
prohibit the use within her own borders, as being
herself a land of Peace. But having an eye to
the protection of trade and the encouragement of
commerce, and in no wise allowing sentiment to
meddle with business, she laughed within her
sleeve and winked within her heart, while much
deploring in public the wickedness of evil men,
and did quietly suffer these manufactures to the
injury of Tadt. For Dollarosa was indeed quite the
most remarkable of the nations, and quite the
least particular."

Binko had now gathered round him a band of
discontented and turbulent spirits who made
themselves feared far and wide under the name of
Binko's Blues, and cruised in a big ironclad called
the *Tonic Bark*. They dressed in blue from head
to foot, and at meal times they wore each a blue
rosette in his coat in mockery of a prevailing
custom in Tadt, where one Phœbus Apollinaris, the
chief of the party called the Sentimentals, had

during a period of holding office carried a Blue
Rosette Bill which forbade the introduction of
any strong drink into the kingdom, and made
every Tadtite wear a blue rosette in sign of
obedience. If he or she was seen without one,
he or she was banished. Phœbus Apollinaris
was considered a very liberal-minded statesman,
which enabled him to insist upon everybody
agreeing with him for everybody's own good.
But the bill made Binko very angry indeed, and
he drank more nig than ever when he heard of
it: though at the same time it did him a good
deal of service in his trade, which of course
combined smuggling with the other branches of
piracy. For a good deal of strong drink was still
secretly consumed in Tadt. Binko himself had
discarded all the outward marks of a pirate,
such as turbans and sashes and the like, and for
distinction dressed always in a tall black hat, new
and glossy, and in a well-fitting frock coat and
continuations of the same colour. He did this
for a reason; for his life was of course of much

F

more importance than those of his followers, and
his costume made him less conspicuous. He
suspended a large scimitar in a strap round his
waist, and carried a stout revolver in his breast
pocket, stock upwards for fear of accidents. But
being liable to losing his temper so frequently, he
generally carried a thick gold-headed stick for
immediate use.

One important episode in Binko's previous
history (for you see I am still leading up to
my narrative) must not be forgotten, as it gave
a sharper edge to his hatred of order and his
hostility to the reigning family in Tadt. There
was a time, as I have said, when the Sentimentals were in office, and as their policy was based
upon a belief in the universal goodness of
everybody if you would only trust them, (except
with drink,) they declared that Binko was very
ill-used in being kept out of the country, (this was
while Floriline's father was still young and reigning, and there was no danger to the succession,)
and had him pardoned for his piracies and brought

back. Thereupon he was immediately elected a member of the Uncommons by a very Republican town somewhere in Tadt. Now no member was admitted to the debates of the Uncommons before he had taken an oath that he was a good man, and did not covet other men's goods; and there was much curiosity as to how Binko would go through it. "Can you swear, sir?" said the Krelc,* or officer, of the candidate when he came up. "Can I swear?" shouted Binko in a deep bass, his face turning a still deeper purple. Then rising immediately into his other voice he shrieked out such an appalling volley of bad language, obviously picked up at sea, that the Krelc turned pale and fled; the whole Uncommons rose at once to its legs and denounced the offender; the strongest of the attendant beef-eaters seized him by the collar, and though severely bitten and kicked in the process succeeded in expelling him from the place; and a bill was brought in that very evening without any notice, and passed in all its forms that night, to receive the royal assent before breakfast the next morning, to prevent anybody from ever swearing more than once in the course of a debate. The Goroos combined with the Ministry (the Sentimentals) to try to throw it out, calling it the Binko Revenge Bill because it was to act backwards as well as forwards. Blocus, a casual member of the Uncommons notorious for objecting to everything, rushed from an excellent dinner to object to that. But it was useless. The Thigs and Wories combined in universal wrath; the Sentimentals were expelled from office on the spot amid a general outcry; and Binko was once more banished from the country to go back to his evil ways, breathing vows of vengeance, (which became serious to think of when it appeared that there was to be no king to reign in Tadt,) and carrying off with him to Dollarosa an unusually large number of Tadtite works of fiction, to receive for them an unusually large commission from the Dollarosan publishers.

CHAPTER III.

WHEN the Lord Honidhu's decision was finally
given, everything became unsettled and threatening in Tadt. The Binko party, which was said
to be strong in the Republican towns for no
particular reason, (because, of course, Binko
would have to be a king quite as much as
anybody else, and indeed rather more so,)
went about with a great many processions and
banners, and held all sorts of meetings in all
sorts of places, where everybody applauded
everything that was said tremendously, and

agreed that the name of Tadt was never in such
bad 'repute as it was now, but did nothing after
all.   Binko cruised about in the *Tonic Bark*,
expecting to be generally invited to become
king at once according to the Sallic Law; but
the matter did not go much beyond meetings,
and there seemed on the whole to be a general
determination to keep Binko out, law or no law.
Happily for the party of order who formed the
great majority of the country, an entirely new
point of law was soon discovered which settled
the whole thing.   The Sallic Law was carefully
looked into by the authorities, and was found to
be so loosely worded, (a most unusual thing with
laws,) that after all it only applied to the
original case of Aunt Sally herself; and another
law of the same kind would have to be passed
to make Binko king, and to shut out pretty
Princess Floriline, called the Fragrant from the
extraordinary sweetness of her disposition.   A
few enthusiastic Binkites introduced the Binko
Succession Bill accordingly; but it met with a

disgust as general as the favour with which the
Binko Revenge Bill had been received, and was
thrown out of the Uncommons as vigorously as
the man had been himself. It was certain that
Binko was not a very popular person in Tadt.
One proposal was made at one time by which
all difficulties seemed likely to be arranged;
namely that a marriage should take place between Binko and Floriline as soon as she was
old enough. She was at the time only seven:
but then he was not more than forty, and
therefore quite in his first youth, according to
the accepted ages of public men in Tadt. He
had a future before him; and his determined
opposition to the Blue Rosette Bill gained him
a good many secret friends upon public grounds,
even amongst those who most disliked his
character.

The queen-mother Helenamaia, however, entirely
declined to have anything at all to say to what she
called this monstrous proposal, and a chivalrous
party of young Tadtites gave her an earnest and

enthusiastic support. The Princess Floriline became
a popular pet with everybody, except the discontented people who always object to everything, and
when the decision was at last given by which she
was to succeed to the throne when she should come
of age at sweet seventeen, there never had been
so much rejoicing heard of. The number of bon-
fires that were burnt, the number of oxen that
were roasted whole, the barrels of new national
drinks, enodeoz,* enozodeh,* and claregnig,* which
were consumed upon the premises, exceeded in
amount all that was ever known. It was whispered
moreover, that Binko himself, who always had an
eye to business, even when his feelings were most
hurt, made the largest profit out of contraband
liquors of an old-fashioned and forbidden kind
which he had ever yet made at one time. Certainly
the number of charges at the police courts, of what
was now called " unwonted excitement," and pun-
ishable accordingly (drunkenness having been
abolished) was quite unusual. Enodeoz never got
into so many heads before.

Ten years went peacefully by upon their course after this, during which the development of the form and character of the Princess Floriline was watched by the whole country with the most affectionate interest. She was wonderfully educated with all the latest improvements, and her health managed according to the strictest sanitary regulations. Whether she felt hungry or not, she had always one egg with her toast for breakfast, and either a slice of cold meat or one small mutton chop for luncheon, and fish, joint, and a plain pudding (once of each) for dinner, neither less nor more. Kensal-à-Green, the chief court physician, was very particular about this, and every year he wrote down on a sheet of paper the exact programme of her diet and exercise, which looked like the dinner list at a coffee house. Kensal-à-Green always did this for all his patients, and the programmes were all nearly the same for all of them, whatever their sex, bulk, or occupation. For it was not so necessary that the programme should be made to suit them, as that they should be made to suit it, like a famous bed

G

in the classics which everybody had to lie in,
whether he was short or long. No difference was
even made by the famous court physician in the
Princess's case, except that her programme was
written out on satin, and had gilt round the edges.
But she assured her guardians that the cold mutton
at luncheon did not taste a bit the better for that.
I am almost afraid to tell you about Floriline's
education. All the principal members of the Sage-
green Committee were consulted about it in turn,
and the highest modern standard was preserved.
In music, she was carefully kept from the sight of
anything that had anything like a tune in it, and
was committed for that purpose to the especial care
of the Hair-Professor Shpex, whose country had
been the first to abolish tunes as foolish and
frivolous things. Under the same tutor she pursued her inquiries into the origin of the Tadt-Pole,
and frequently visited (in a diving-bell) the spot
where it originally stood, till her curly little head
grew quite full of suppressed learning, and it was
a wonder how the curls kept their shape. But they

did, and curled so rebelliously close to her brown
head that when she woke in the mornings it looked
like a little sea, and all the efforts of the royal
nursery maids could scarcely make it respectable.
In art, Floriline was only allowed to paint the
limpest subjects which could be found for her, upon
the principle that flatness was the true line of
beauty, which made it the more provoking that she
herself insisted upon growing up with a decided
tendency to plumpness, which was likely to prevent
her being admired by the people whose opinion
upon those points was desirable. In poetry, she
was only allowed what she could not understand;
for nothing was poetry which she could. Her
reading upon general subjects was confined to the
pages of the two great Sage-green magazines, the
Present Sentry and the *Nightlightly Review*, whose
titles showed how wide awake they were about
everything. They were originally introduced into
Tadt by Shpex and his friends, and their motto was
a passage from an old Karamsinian comedy. It
was that "Every kind of subject was permitted,

as long as it was tedious." Anything at all entertaining was strictly excluded, because of its bad
effects upon the mind ; but partly also because so
many people in Tadt lived by writing, and so few
of them had the smallest power of entertaining
anybody, that it would never do to set a bad
example. Articles which nobody but their writers
could understand were much in request, and those
which the writers did not understand themselves
were paid for extra. I should tell you—as in
writing a correct history there is nothing like
being correct—that all this happened before the
change in the system of education in Tadt which I
described in the first chapter. Indeed the questions
arising out of the lessons which Floriline had to
learn had a great deal to do with the change. For
the truth is that the young lady rebelled, and the
common sense of the country with her. She had a
quick wit and a bright nature of her own, and
wanted amusement as flowers want the sun, or did
until it was discovered that they could get on as
well with the electric light. So when she got tired

of her lessons she did what was very wrong and
nobody could indeed have thought possible. She
took the Sage-green Committee in ! She learned
for herself some simple little ballads with nothing
but a tune in them, and sang them out of school-
hours in a way which made her particular friends,
who kept the secret, laugh and cry. She drew
the most delightful little caricatures of the Committee and Shpex, not agreeing at all with any line of
beauty, but astonishing likenesses for all that. She
managed to go to the theatre in disguise, and laugh
with all her might at the fairy operas of the witty
and frivolous Brothers Pinaphor, after reading the
Nightlightly during her afternoon nap ; and last
and worst, she got from a circulating library several
volumes of novels in paper covers, and written in
the Cimarosian language, which was forbidden in
all the schools established by the Sage-green Committee. The Cimarosians were a very witty and
amusing people, as ready to laugh or be laughed at
as the Karamsinians were neither one nor the other,
and wrote upon all subjects in such easy and simple

language that it wasn't worth understanding. Some of their books were not very good reading certainly, but then there was no occasion to read them, and as Floriline was a very nice girl, you may be quite sure she didn't.

So human nature came to the top as usual, and Floriline the Fragrant grew up exactly that—a very nice girl. The Sage-green Committee had not succeeded in inventing anything nicer than that, though they did a great deal to spoil many promising specimens. She was adored in the palace and worshipped in the country, and the people used to throw down flowers for her to walk upon when she went out. And when she reached the age of seventeen and was crowned queen (her mother Helenamaia died some years earlier) the rejoicings were even greater than they had been ten years before. There was a special meeting of the Sage-green Committee to discuss whether Tadt could be any more called a kingdom now there was no king, and the opinion of the Crown lawyers was asked whether it mightn't legally be called a queendom.

QUEEN FLORILINE THE FRAGRANT.

All the Thig lawyers said it must, and all the Wory lawyers that it mustn't, and as the Wories were in, a kingdom it was still called. And while the Sage-green Committee held their meeting about the young queen, another important body of people held theirs too; and they were the fairies. For in spite of learning and progress and everything else there were still fairies in Tadt, for the people who knew where to look for them.

CHAPTER IV.

THE FAIRY WARNING.

NOTHING in the world, I believe, can ever banish those dear and wonderful little people altogether. They have lived so long in all sorts of books and stories, and have made so many mossy nooks and babbling streams alive with their adventures, that not all the railways and chimneys in or out of Fairyland can ever quite get rid of them. It is true that their playgrounds have become smaller and more limited of choice than they used to be; that they often fly from the harvest lands and the ears of corn in which they loved to nestle, at the shriek of the ugly engine whistle

H

and the sight of the big red eyes of the steam monster as he comes lumbering along through their dainty solitudes, with a noisy night-express tied to him like a huge iron kettle to an elephant's tail; and that they shrink as a body further and further away, as the great smoke-circle widens round the towns like the eddy round a stone thrown into the water, and spreads waves of suffocation all about, which the healthy lungs of the fairies cannot bear. Too often, alas! as the big towns and the big improvements grow, they spread their sad little wings and droop their shapely heads, and cast their bright eyes down, and hover about like the bee looking for a flower to settle on. They are imperceptible to men's gross senses, so that they cannot see what they are driving away, nor know how many gentle and faithful friends who have been sweet councillors to them of soft and kindly thoughts, comforters in trouble, and purifiers in joy, bringing rest, rest, rest to the over-anxious brain, and to the toiler too heart-set upon wealth and success, are

melting away from them in search of the purer
air yet to be found, fit for such innocent and
ethereal spirits to breathe and play in. Sometimes in the night the watcher hears them, borne
away to new scenes and distant places on an
invisible rush of wings, and looking out to know
what it may be, fancies that it is nothing but a
moan of wind too faint to stir the trees. And a
sadness falls upon his spirit as if something had
gone out of his life which it is ill to miss; and he
lies down to dream. But for the fairies, they are
immortal. Still in the deep rich heart of the
country, and in the stately solitude of fine old
forests; on the tracts of untro dden rock-bound
sand which sparkle in sunshine or in moonlight in
answer to the sparkle of the sea; where little
undiscovered streams keep the velvet mosses
green round and between the gnarled and knotted
spurs of the protecting oak; where sudden tors
rise and point sharply skyward from the heaving
bosom of the moor, the fairies hold their senate
where none of coarser mould may see and hear,

nor mortal company insult them with the petty
selfish cares with which men are so resolute to
fill and spoil their lives, for all true grace of
profit and of use. Not even mortals, however,
can always drive them away. More even than
other solitudes they love to haunt "the quiet
walks, sweetened by lovers' breath," where they
can track with whispered blessings some young
pair lost in life's best and most unselfish dream,
and earnestly pray that, for them at least, Love and
Unselfishness may grow up hand-in-hand together.
Their "silver footfalls on the silent ground" are unheard of all but Heaven as they follow in the lovers'
wake; still for all slips of ours the guardians and
best friends of man. Still in those mysterious
senates they discuss the cases of good men lost and
earnest in the mid-current of the fighting crowd;
and despatch some tiny deputation to bring
unguessed comfort to his hearth, and nestle at his
side as divine ambassadors. At the wealthy
merchant's work, at the clerk's monotonous round
of ill-paid daily toil, in my lady's oriel window, or

at the seamstress's attic-pane, by those most
favoured and least favoured too of the outward
grace of Fortune, in all the dreariest centres of
grinding labour and of stifling smoke, they can yet
be present, and they are—wherever the magnetism
of a single heart and a true life may all unknowing
summon them. Where those are not, there neither
are they. Poverty in itself is no passport to
their entrance ; and wealth in itself no bar. And
even as Truth and Love purify the gloomiest
surroundings till the thickest atmosphere grows
fit for them to breathe, so over their best beloved
sylvan and moorland solitudes the air grows
poisonous and heavy, and the scent of the haw-
thorn and the wild-rose sickens and droops away,
at the skulk of a traitor's foot, or the whisper of
a lying lover. If what I have told you seems
something of a contradiction, it must be because
you must understand that the fairies are very
contradictory little people ; but if you can use
your eyes to see what my humble parable means,
you will know how it is that there are still, as I

said at the end of my last chapter, fairies in Tadt, and for that matter, everywhere else, for those who know where to look for them.

For those who did, and could therefore report the proceedings, there was an enormous gathering of fairies met together to do honour to the young Queen Floriline. It was so enormous that, small as the fairies were, it was impossible to find room for them all; and though those who came first put down their hats on all the mushrooms and toad-stools there in order to keep them for seats, no sooner had they turned their backs than they found that later comers had sat upon their hats, and so taken their places, in defiance of all the rules of the Fairy Parliament. The hill upon which they met was the most solitary mountain in all Tadt, and was called after the primroses which grew upon it in such profusion. It had once been the most frequented place in Kashburg, (especially on Sundays,) for it was really in the capital; but soon after the passing of the Blue Rosette Bill, and the improved habits of the people in consequence,

Phœbus Apollinaris and his friends found out that it would be much better for them to stay at home and read nice improving books on Sundays, than wander about in search of fresh air and foolish amusements. So the merry-go-rounds and the refreshment booths were all sternly and properly put down, open air on Sundays was strictly forbidden, the front doors and shutters were all shut everywhere, and the most excellent and serious conversation was carried on inside for twenty-four hours without any interruption. So the fairies took advantage of this, and had the mountain all to themselves on Sunday, though it was said that they did not at all approve of rules of that kind, and even used to leave the loveliest little casks of mountain-dew at the houses of their particular favourites on their way home at night, without saying a word to anybody about it.

The fairies, there is no doubt upon the matter, were exceedingly fond of the young Queen Floriline. No amount of tutors and masters, nor even the shocking deceits which as I have told you she used to practise upon them, could avail to keep them away from her. At her christening they danced in secret all about the font, lighting up pretty tapers in the church which only their friends the angels saw, and tickling the nose of the Cardinal-Archbishop of Kashburg with straws when he made the ceremony too long for the future queen's patience, and made her cry, so that he sneezed in the middle of his discourse, and had to cut it short half way through, instead of improving the occasion as he had fully intended. Two particularly gentle and pretty old fairies, (and in fairydom, as in humanity, nothing is more pleasant to the view than a gentle and a pretty old lady,) whose names were Mother Wit and Mother Tongue, presided over this airy congress, and gave this god-child of their best. One attendant fairy hovered over the pretty head, all round which the nicest hair in the world was beginning to grow like down, and touched it with a particularly tempting kind of golden dye of which only the fairies had the receipt, so that it grew up of a wonderful natural colour which all the ladies of the court tried to imitate in vain. Another thinking that the baby's nose was likely to be too classically straight, tipped it up at the end just in the slightest possible way, and stuck it in its new place with a fairy-gum which was exactly what was wanted, and made it for ever afterwards the most bewitching and irresistible little nose which was ever seen upon the face of a queen or anybody else. A third secretly produced a fairy-needle which she always carried with her, (to sit on the blunt end when she was tired,) and pricked in the middle of the royal baby's chin such a perfect dimple, that no dimple was ever known like it. All the fairy godmothers out of all the fairy-stories brought her all the good qualities they could find to give her for presents, and there was not a single bad fairy there to interfere with the ceremony, or make any · thing unpleasant. Indeed there was no such thing as a bad fairy in Tadt ; for if there ever were any, they had long, long ago been driven out of the

I

land. And one fairy there was who slipped a talisman into the little baby-fingers, which closed tight upon it as such little fingers do, after a vigorous but vain attempt to hit out straight into the face of the Cardinal-Archbishop, when he showed signs of using more water, and being more tedious, than the child thought necessary. The talisman turned out, when Baby's hand was afterwards unclasped by the united efforts of several nurses, to be a quaint and beautiful coral ring which exactly fitted the fourth finger, and grew larger or smaller with it ever afterwards exactly as she grew plumper or more slender, so that everybody knew that it must have a magic power of some kind, and even the Sage-green Committee could never tell what to make of it. During her days of baby-hood the Princess crowed so loud when it was put on, and kicked so hard when it was taken off, that everybody soon had a superstitious belief in it, and she was allowed to wear it always. And one day during her girlhood when there was nobody near her except Shpex, who had just been giving her a lesson in which he proved positively that nothing ever did or could happen out of the ordinary way, which could not be explained to be the most natural thing in the world, a sweet clear voice belonging to nobody whispered in her ear, " When you are in real and great danger, and cannot keep yourself awake, and he whom you shall love best shall be by your side and in the same danger, turn the coral ring thrice on your finger, call steadily three times three on the name of the Fairy Robur, and do not be afraid ! " And of that strange fairy warning Floriline whispered no word to anybody, till as time went quietly on she had nearly forgotten all about it.

She had quite forgotten all about it when she was declared queen, and the fairies held high council and festival. She had more than quite forgotten, when in another year or two the time came for her to be married, just as if she had been a pretty girl like anybody else. I need not tell you how many pretenders were found for the

queen's hand, which carried the crown of Tadt in
it. The Uncommons and the Sage-green Committee had several discussions, and decided upon
several eligible husbands, though nobody revived
the proposal about Binko which had been made in
the queen-mother's lifetime. Queen Floriline
meanwhile, showing a will of her own which
caused much uneasiness, (it being very doubtful
by law if she had any business to have one,) looked
at all the photographs of all the eligible gentlemen,
and then refused to see any of the originals. It
was pointed out to her that photographs were not
always like; but she said that they must be quite
like enough to prevent her wishing to see the
people they were taken from. Whether the fairies,
who among themselves kept on holding their own
meetings on the subject in their own way, ever
whispered advice in her sleeping ear, or put pretty
and honest thoughts into her true and womanly
heart, can never be said for certain. But it is
certain that something or somebody, having no
connexion whatever with the Sage-green Committee,

or the Uncommons, or the *Present Sentry*, or any
known source of light and leading, perhaps the
very voice which had long ago whispered that
half-forgotten warning, kept on saying at all sorts
of odd times and place, in a changeless but musical
tune like the chime of sound church bells—
" Floriline, Floriline, marry for love." And so it
came about that when she was not yet twenty
years old, it became known through the length and
breadth of Tadt that Queen Floriline had exercised
her royal prerogative to a purpose by choosing for
herself, and that she was going to be married!
And now I have come round once more, like the
Hair-Professor, exactly to where I began : and I
tell you again as I have told you three times
before, that there was, just upon this account,
great excitement in the kingdom of Tadt.

CHAPTER V.

THE Cocoa-grounds of Mara-Villa were gay with flags and arches, on the day when Queen Floriline the Fragrant was married to the Baron Osy. Mara-Villa was the queen's favourite home, a charming country retreat, far from the noise and smoke of the great city, and situate on one of the most smiling and beautiful of the bays which the sea forms in picturesque variety round the coasts of Tadt. The most perfect art had been shown in the laying out of the grounds, which were called the Cocoa-grounds because the prevailing colour and tone of the decorations was a rich and tasty chocolate. The carpets and the curtains, the frames of the pictures and the bindings of the books, the papers which lined the walls and ceilings, and all the mantelpieces and fireplaces, chairs, sofas, candlesticks, chintzes and sofa-covers, were of the same soft and reposeful hue. The whole thing had been designed by the eminent court painter whom you have already heard of as having some years before exhibited at the Ymcdaca his celebrated picture of Binko's moustache and nose, as a " Lunacy in Red and White." The idea was carried out with artistic completeness out of doors, where all the arches and urns, and statues and imitation ruins, and out-houses and boat-houses and stables and arbours and kiosks and steps and gasometers, were of the same shade. In autumn, during the fall of the leaf, the effect was quite complete. The idea had been first suggested to the harmonious soul of the artist, when consulted as to the decorations, by the necessity of living up to the big cocoa tree which grew in the centre of the grounds, and, by an ingenious mechanical contrivance

grafted upon nature, supplied the refreshing drink
which the plant distils, ready made in luxurious
abundance. The one tree did the whole thing:
from the original cocoa-nut which grew at its
base the operation of growing, grinding, boiling, and
supplying with milk and sugar in exact proportions,
proceeded inside the trunk, and every little leaf
formed a hidden cocoa-fountain. You had but
to press a spring which bubbled up hard by, and
streams of delicious drink spurted from the
leaves in abundance, without danger of inebria-
tion. Elegant cups of china and porcelain were
nailed in layers against the walls of all the
adjoining arbours, and could be removed for use
with a little trouble. It was recognised in Tadt
that walls were the proper place for cups and
saucers, and in the most artistic houses the
pictures were always laid upon the breakfast-tables,
to give them a cheerful aspect. Often and often
while the beautiful maids of honour and the
well-proportioned pages of the queen's attractive
court disported themselves among the square

grass-plots and rectangular walks of the villa gardens, would a maiden's playful hand press the obedient spring, and deluge some unsuspecting companion with the warm and innocent liquid. With a peal of silvery laughter, her moistened garments and short but variegated petticoats clinging picturesquely to her fine form, the victim of the pleasantry would retire in sweet confusion, to change her things. The days of that fair court passed by in a round of innocent pleasures. Sometimes they sang lively choruses to lilting tunes, standing some twenty in a row of alternate youths and maids, with costumes of different colours, picturesquely assorted and cunningly arranged by the master-mind of the Director of the Ceremonies. The short and starry tunic of the boy, his shapely leg clad in closely-fitting silken hose, contrasted pleasantly to the eye with the fantastic skirts, well-nigh as brief as the tunic, which his girlish neighbour would ever and again smooth down with dainty gesture. And it was delightful to see the motley throng,

K

as each verse of the inspiring ditty ended, break by a wholesome and unanimous instinct into the steps of some strange wild dance, which seemed to serve at once the purposes of courtly recreation and strong muscular exercise. Anon, when the youths and maids were weary of the sport, a band af athletes would vary the monotony by a series of feats on poles or on trapezes, at which the laughing court looked on. The strains of an invisible orchestra accompanied the while from underneath the ground, while a privileged few surveyed the scene with strong field-glasses from the galleries of the villa, the rich chocolate background lending a mellow dignity to the whole. It was the very gaiety of Fairyland.

Never had the maids and pages of Floriline the Fragrant's court enjoyed themselves so thoroughly as they did upon their young mistress's wedding-day. It was a lovely day in June, when everything was at its best. The birds sang carols of their own, composed for the occasion, upon every tree in the neighbourhood : the roses and the

strawberries and the asparagus vied with each
other in their different perfections. The sea at
the bottom of the cocoa-grounds was like a silver
looking-glass laid at Floriline's feet as a wedding-
present from the fairies; and those little people
were busying themselves unseen everywhere,
perching on daisies and riding on sunbeams,
filling acorn-cups with cocoa from the tree for
their own private drinking, and whispering all
the softest fancies in the ears of the pretty
maids of honour about those whom they loved
the best, till they tingled again at the confidence,
and from their own coral pink turned as red
as the scarlet maples, whose great spreading
branches opened out as if they wanted to embrace
the whole island for the occasion. There was,
indeed, a great deal of embracing done, for the
loves of Osy and Floriline were infectious
throughout the merry court, and the numbers
of marriages which were announced to follow the
royal wedding became quite an annoyance to the
Registrar-General.

But it is a melancholy fact that a silver cloud
has generally a black lining. There was a
proverb to that effect which was very well known
in Tadt, a country which had a great store of
remarkable proverbs. "It's a wise father that
knows his own child"—a deep saying, invented
by an early Binkite when the effects of the Sallic
Law were upset by the birth of an unexpected
Hoppo, to suggest that he wasn't real, had long
passed into the language. "The early worm
destroys the birds," "Those who throw stones
shouldn't live in glass houses," "Marry at leisure
and repent in haste," and other excellent precepts
of the same kind for the guidance of the young,
were constantly in the mouths of their pastors and
masters. So it was that while everybody was
still in the beautiful church on the summit of
the grounds, to listen to the blessing pronounced
upon the Princess Floriline and the Baron Osy
by the Cardinal-Archbishop of Kashburg; while
the anthems were softly and beautifully pealing
round the fretted ceiling and the emblazoned

walls, where the faces of defunct kings of Tadt (Echoes and Hoppoes many in number, but possessed of a strong family resemblance) looked down out of sculptured niches over the carved stalls of the Knights of the Order (without which no free admission could be obtained) ; while our friends the fairies hovered, dainty and invisible, under the direction of Mother Wit and Mother Tongue, round the rich military uniforms of the men and the rustling silks and satins of the more expensive sex, but especially near the manly but shrinking form of the bridegroom, and the bright soft tresses of the bride ; and while the special correspondents in a private gallery of their own took notes of everything as fast as they could, with an official called the court-guide to tell them who everybody was, and the court-milliner to explain what everybody had on :—while all these things were in progress, I say, two strange men might have been seen with very obvious purposes of concealment about them, wandering stealthily about among the thick growth of bushes

and underwood which sloped suddenly down to
the water's edge at the foot of the cocoa-grounds.
It was afterwards said, when the startling events
of Floriline's wedding-day became matter of
history, and all the newspapers were giving equally
accurate but entirely different accounts of them,
that many strange and ominous circumstances
had been noticed on the previous night. A long
and low-lying and rakish-looking craft, bearing in
indistinct letters round the prow, as far as they
could be made out, an inscription like " *The Tonic
Bark*," and iron-clad, because iron was the strongest
form of tonic, had been seen to cruise in the
offing. Curiously-manned boats had landed knots
of curiously-dressed men, all in blue, at the various
public-houses which were built at regular intervals
along the coast for the purposes of refreshment and
defence, upon temperance principles—suspended
for the joyous occasion. Some of these men had
taken up their quarters for the night on shore.
They were affable, but did not mix freely, except
their liquors. They held strange conferences in

corners, and whispered in audible voices allusions to "to-morrow" which would have excited suspicion in anybody but the innocent; and seldom parted one from the other, even for the moment, without a vigorous grip of the hand and a remark of "Ha ha!" in suppressed but powerful tones. A good deal of mild excitement was created among the villagers by these mysterious occurrences on the eve of their Queen's wedding-day: but the strangers consumed drink so freely, and gave so many orders of different kinds in the neighbourhood, that they were set down as generally good for trade, and no notice of anything unusual was given up at the Villa, or country palace of the Queen. Afterwards, when it all came out in evidence upon the full inquiry that was held, it was decided that there had been a good deal of carelessness somewhere, and the decision was even confirmed upon appeal by the Lord Honidhu himself. But here I am a little anticipating the course of True History.

CHAPTER VI.

INTRODUCING MUCH FINE COMPANY.

OF the two strangers who might have been seen among the bushes of the cocoa-grounds, one was short and round and fiery of face, and dressed in a black suit with a tall black hat. He might have seen fifty summers, (and consequently one winter less or more, according to the month he was born in,) or he might not: for it is always safer to use the conditional mood when one desires to be accurate. His companion was middle-aged, and dressed but seedily; and he was tall and thin and pale, and apparently oppressed with the weight of a permanent melancholy. His remarks when he spoke were short and to the point, and very sententious; indeed at times almost commonplace. But it was clear to the observer that he had a great influence over the mind of his companion.

"We have landed, captain," he observed sadly, "just in time to be too late."

"'Tis so indeed," growled his companion in tones hoarse with suppressed pain. "She is another's. They always are. And what other's? What did they tell us his infernal name was?" The speaker seldom used a substantive of any kind without one or more very strong adjectives attached to it, which may for the most part be left to the imagination.

"The Baron Osy," suggested the other.

"Where does he come from?"

"From Ankworks. He is the Baron Osy de Ankworks. He came a-courting every Thursday, and returned on the Sunday morning."

"Is he rich?"

"Very."

"But not so rich as I am. I have made millions on this last trip, which finished just too late. I have adored that girl since first I set eyes upon her, and for her sake I have been amassing all this wealth in trade!"

"Slave-trade, captain!"

"What does that matter? All trades are alike now a days. Only make the money, and nobody will ask you how it was done." The voice of the speaker was swelling into a roar. "O Tadtite mothers, hear me"—he was proceeding.

"They all will hear you if you shout in that way," said the younger man placidly; and his tones acted like a sedative upon the irritated nerves of Binko; for he indeed it was. With a mighty effort at self-control he succeeded in collecting himself, as a visible spasm quivered through his closely-fitting frock coat, while the tall black hat shook with emotion.

"You are right, Odonto," he said; and seating himself upon the nearest bush he began to weep like a child.

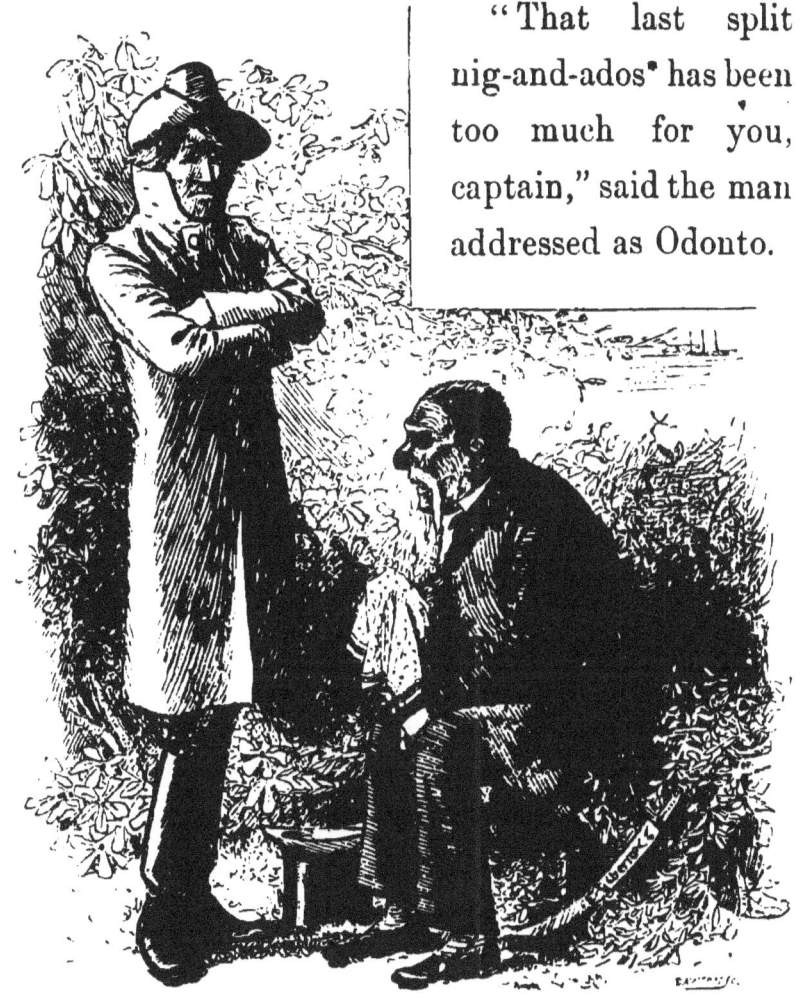

"That last split nig-and-ados* has been too much for you, captain," said the man addressed as Odonto.

AND SEATING HIMSELF ON THE NEAREST BUSH HE BEGAN TO WEEP LIKE A CHILD.

"Lieutenant, be careful, or you may go too far," Binko answered, warningly. "You have had troubles, but I have never suggested that you owed them to drink."

"No," murmured Odonto. "I owe drink to them: and for that I am grateful. I was the King of Lavradio, I was, and with my two brothers, Kalydor and Macassar, divided the whole Empire of Rowland the Great. The ivory kingdom fell to my share; and I thought myself securely seated on its famous throne, (which screws upwards and backwards at any angle,) when my subjects grew weary of me and called me out of date: and Floriline the Fragrant has annexed the Ivory Kingdom. They attacked me in all the newspapers. I had to fly for my life; and I am the lieutenant of a pirate-bark." He sank down upon another bush and groaned, as memory became too much for him.

"You are the very man for my purpose," ground Binko from between his teeth. "I know your wrongs, and you know mine. What do I pay you for?"

"You never do pay me, captain," answered the other.

"But I perquisite you!" promptly exclaimed Binko, "I perquisite you richly, and I bestow upon you my personal friendship. More—I am showing you the way to your revenge and to

THE HAUNT OF THE FAIRIES.

your crown. Once let Floriline and her lands be mine, and Tadt restores to you the Ivory Kingdom (or I tell you so till I get it," he added apart). "She is always annexing, but I will teach her more honest ways."

"Floriline is now another's, as you said."

"What of that? I take her from that other. I have sworn by port and starboard that she shall be mine, and she shall! There are times when I forget myself—"

"There are, captain!"

"But never my vow. I thought I had timed things rightly, and would that I had disappointed this coxcomb of his bridal! I have come too late to marry her now, for bigamy is not permitted, and law is supreme. But——"

"Another man's wife is often better than one's own," commented Odonto.

"Right you are!" exclaimed his excited chief. "Little do these reckless feasters dream who is near them. I have taken all my measures as well as the court-tailor! Six trusty Blues lie in ambush at the nearest public, wetting their whistles till I blow mine! Six more man the *Cockle-Shell* (which reduces when the *Bark* is too strong, and the *Bark* is close at hand). The happy pair will be sure to dismiss their

court ere long, and spoon in the garden! Then
out we spring and seize them, for I will make
that Osy a very slave on board my bark, and
off we go together. Osy shall die by inches."

"Or swing from yards. It's shorter."

"On the contrary; inches are shorter than
yards. And I propose to gloat. When he is
dead I marry his widow, and return with her
to claim the throne, which till then will remain
in commission! Have I not planned it well?"

"You have a head, captain. It is a pity that
so many things get into it."

"Love and revenge have driven them all out.
How dared that minx reject the heart of Binko?
Never shall she or anybody sport with me thus.
I'll choke the bridegroom with the nuptial tie,
and wring the parson's neck with his own altar.
Let me get at them. Let me pass!" and he
grew excited as Odonto restrained him.

"You can't pass for sterling coin to-day,"
said the lieutenant, "you haven't got the ring.
And hark," he added, "the bells!" as a merry

silver peal rang out from the height. "Let us
be discreet for the moment."

"We will," replied the pirate, "indeed, we
must. But those bells shall talk in quite another
chime and tune, before I've done with them!"
And even as he spoke the two ominous figures
made themselves scarce, and crouched among
the heather, while a very different set of faces
appeared upon the scene.

Never did the charming pages and maidens of
Queen Floriline's maiden court look so charming
as upon that happy day. New costumes had
been made for them all, even more bewitchingly
attractive than usual. New songs had been
studied and new dances arranged; and wonderful
combinations of colour flashed upon the spectator
like the changes in a kaleidoscope. The whole
court and all the guests came from the ceremony in well-ordered procession, and everybody
who was anybody was there. The special correspondents, writing as fast as they could, began

to lose themselves in descriptions of reseda velvet, of ostrich-feathers, of amethyst robes and jupes of poult, of airy and diaphanous tissues of strange and divers material, and gave the court-guide and the court-milliner a great deal of trouble in correcting their articles. It literally rained dukes and marquises—the Sage-Green Committee were there in force and in spectacles, through which they might behold the Ministers and the Opposition jostle each other in quite a friendly way—and all the celebrities of the hour walked in the procession by twos and twos, preceded in each instance by an official called a sandwich-man, who served the treble purpose of supplying light refreshment on the march, of blowing tunes upon a trumpet of brass before the celebrity he was appointed to wait upon, and of bearing that gentleman's name upon the paste-board suit which was the uniform of the sand-wich-men, in huge letters, richly emblazoned both before and behind. When at times the sandwich-men grew tired of blowing on the

L

brass trumpets, the critics and the special correspondents, who were close at hand everywhere,
would relieve them of their instruments, and
blow a lively blast ; and if they too became a
little out of breath, sometimes the celebrity
would with his own hands condescend to take
up the trumpet, and blow it for himself
rather than that there should be an interval of
silence.

Thus it was, that with long flowing hair
confined by a yellow ribbon, and with trowsers
of rich green velvet reaching to the knee, from
which downwards the lower leg was cased in
stockings of red—smiling with much kindness
upon the laughing maidens of the court—and
showering upon the crowd versicles of his own
upon rather loose sheets, which luckily were
not easy to understand, came the court-poet
Lilliflop.

Another remarkable figure in the procession was
the court-tragedian Monopol, or the Only One.
IIis was a fine keen face, and a curious manner and

expression. His hair, like Lilliflop's, was long and dreamy as a woman's, and about the man there

LILLIFLOP.

was a singular magnetism which much affected men and women both, and caused him to be much flattered in public and much run down in private,

L 2

(except by his real friends) as was the most
unusual habit of the world in which my story
happened.   What was oddest about him was
this : that he seemed to quiet observers to have,
while in private something reserved and reticent
and modest, a keen sense of fun of his own as
to the real worth of all the trumpet-blowing that
went on in the court of Floriline.   When he
took up the blowing of his own trumpet as I
have described it, it was with a curious wink of
the eye and an odd smile about the mouth,
which suggested to those same observers (of
whom there were not many in Tadt) that he
knew more than he much cared to say.   And it
is a fact that, in varying degrees, the same
seemed generally true of the chief celebrities in
the procession.   Lilliflop was by no means want-
ing in the same humorous quality; conspicuous
also in the good Lord Honidhu and the Master-
Painter Count Sapo-de-Pears, who walked arm-
in-arm in the procession, crowned with roses,
and waving images of silver in the form of

boats which contained pure and flowing butter

WAVING IMAGES OF SILVER IN THE FORM OF BOATS, WHICH CONTAINED
PURE AND FLOWING BUTTER.

with which at intervals they playfully sprinkled
each other. Indeed this form of butter-throwing

was an important part of all Tadtite ceremonies;
and so much of this national farm-produce was
thrown upon Monopol, that his steadiness under
it was quite remarkable.

But I will not dwell at any greater length
on the accessory figures in this wedding procession, when all eyes were turned upon the two
principal performers, whom it was all about.
The Baron Osy de Ankworks was in all respects
a handsome and attractive young man, worthy
the love of a goddess, to say nothing of a queen :
and though not himself in the absolute possession of a crown—for the Barony of Ankworks
did not lay claim to that honour—he was nobly
descended from a very famous line of kings and
legislators, whose origin was lost in the mists
of antiquity. No better king-consort for Queen
Floriline and Tadt could have been found anywhere outside the map : and on the happy day
everybody seemed to think so. The fair maid
of honour Jetoline was a little spiteful about
it to her companion Glykaline, as even maids

of honour will be sometimes : and only the intervention of the sweet Euchrisma (Floriline's favourite) had prevented a battle-royal between the two damsels. For it was freely whispered at court that Jetoline had herself at first attracted the notice of the Baron on one of his weekly visits, before he was induced to raise his eyes as high as the throne itself. So it was that—on somebody among the maidens (before church) remarking that the wedding-dress was exquisitively fitted to the fair bride, and another who was weary of the needle saying that so it ought to be, she had tried it on so often— Jetoline said with a toss of her pretty head that " she didn't think much of the way the queen ' tried it on,' to catch nothing better than a Baron. A queen to go and marry a simple peer ! " she added, with a provoking nose turned upwards.

" My dear," said Glykaline, " peers are gentle and not simple ; and a queen may marry a subject if she likes."

"He is not a subject for congratulation, then, if he marries above his rank," Jetoline answered.

"If nobody should ever marry above that," observed Glykaline, pensively, "why did you try to catch the Baron?"

"I didn't!"

"Oh, you did!"

"I didn't! I didn't! Or if I did," added Jetoline, changing her ground, "so did you if it comes to that. I know——"

"No you don't know," was the answer. "For you did all you knew at the time."

Little was heard after this but a suppressed scuffle, and a murmur of "Let me get at her," promptly checked by a laughing page, who, being very good looking, soothed the irritated feelings of the pretty Jetoline with something which sounded like a kiss, though nobody could say for certain. And when the fair Euchrisma had thrown some of her oil upon the troubled waters in the exercise of her duties as first maid of honour, the little episode was soon forgotten. Such little

breezes among the fair sex would sometimes stir
even the enchanted branches of the cocoa-tree.

JETOLINE AND THE PAGE ALARMED.

The little scene had been long over before the
arrival of the procession from church, with Floriline, a picture of everything lovely and defying

description, leaning in tender trustfulness upon her handsome young husband's arm.

"He does look most dreadfully conceited," whispered Jetoline to her neighbour the page, with whom she had now much close conversation.

"Lots of swagger," replied the page, with sympathy. "But he's doocidly good looking, almost good enough for her!"

He too, had secretly loved the queen. They all had. As he spoke, he thought for a moment that he heard a sympathetic groan proceed from a neighbouring bush—a groan which was almost like a grunt, promptly checked by some unseen interference. Jetoline and her page cast a startled glance upon the bush, and clung very closely to each other. But the sound ceased, and they agreed that it was fancy.

CHAPTER VII.

CONTAINS A KING'S SPEECH AND AN ABDUCTION.

"LONG live the happy pair!" was the cry which rent the skies, miraculously mended immediately afterwards. With an infinite grace acknowledging the compliments of the company, the Baron Osy now stepped forward to address them, in his first king's speech. In the intense emotion which possessed him, he spoke at first not very clearly, and his words seemed confused. He was obviously very nervous, and it appeared as if, to honour the occasion, he had studied an address in rhyme, which had got a little mixed up. With the closest attention and the readiest pens, the special

correspondents could make no more of the opening
sentences than this :

> *" Thanks, my childering !*
> *Your cheers and compliments are most bewildering—*
> *I'm sure the proudest moment of my life*
> *Quite unaccustomed bridesmaids lovely wife*
> *And public speaking."*

A loud chorus of "Hear, hear" assisted the
diffident speaker.　Thunders of applause greeted
the royal opening, and not a few shed tears,
whilst others embraced frantically, including Jetoline and her page.

"What eloquence !" murmured Floriline, an intense pride in her heart's choice filling her perfect
eyes.

"It is neat, but scarcely consecutive," said
others encouragingly.　The king-consort's courage
began to return to him.　" I propose to introduce
many changes into this fortunate isle which shall
make her still more fortunate.　After so long a
succession of Echoes and Hoppoes, it could scarcely

be otherwise, or the state would stagnate." (" Hear, hear !" when some admirers of the old dynasty beginning to object, were immediately expelled.) "I trust to be able to do a good deal more of my work for myself than my predecessors are supposed to have done. The gentlemen of the Uncommons will, I trust, be called together less frequently, to confirm the taxes which I hope to impose." ("Darling !" whispered his bride.) "I shall sit with them myself, and vote, without any respect of party, with any party which will give me what I want. Every time I summon them, I shall inform them at once that the position of the country is all that could be wished, and that they needn't trouble themselves to pass any bills or ask any questions. I shall inform them that nobody need ever speak for more than ten minutes at a time, or more than once in a month." (Murmurs in places.) " And it is my firm belief that everything will go on just as well as it does now— indeed that nobody will find out any difference. The army and navy I propose largely to increase,

and the taxes I have decided at once to double.
I——"

At this point a grave spirit of opposition began
to show itself in the meeting. Signs of considerable disturbance were visible, the crowd was
swaying to and fro, and Binko, beside himself
with excitement, gripped his lieutenant in the
bushes with such violence, as visibly to move him.
"Splendid!" he said. "The beggar on horseback
will upset the coach for himself." And his flaming
countenance might have been seen to shine between
the leaves at intervals like a revolving light, if
everybody had not been so occupied. But the
Baron saw his mistake at once, and recognised
that what had gone down very well in the Barony
of Ankworks, where he had it all his own way,
and voted himself with all the different parties in
turn in order to show that he was equally disgusted
with all of them, would never do in Tadt. He
was a thoroughly clever man, and changed his
ground immediately. "*Did* I say increase the army
and navy, and double the taxes?" he exclaimed,

with one hand upon his own heart, and the other round the waist of his queen. "Out upon my nervous tongue, and the excitement of the occasion! I meant reduce the forces and halve the taxes!" In a moment the king-consort had his audience with him. Nobody can ever please everybody; and a few half-pay officers grumbled. But there were very few of that class present, most of them being in the poor-houses, and the grumble was unheard amidst the tokens of general enthusiasm. The Baron Osy took his cue at once, and looking upon the beaming faces round him, he burst into a magnificent eulogy of Tadt and everything connected with it. He declared that there never had been and never could be such a country—so unselfish and retiring and indifferent to mere wealth, and unwilling to think of its own interests. He turned to the Lord Honidhu, and spoke of the Rab in a way which wetted many handkerchiefs, showing what a chivalrous and devoted body it was, and how it never took anything for being so. He made the Master-Painter blush and smile with the expression

of his passionate admiration for Tadtite art, and of
the prices which it fetched in the market, till the
painter waved his hands in gentle deprecation, as
much as to say, " It's all true ; but don't put it in
that way." He looked at the Sage-green Committee,
spoke of the extraordinary march and triumphs of
science, and pointed out to the members what a
pleasure it must be to them to reflect that when they
had learned all the secrets and arrangements of the
solar system, there must, as far as he could see, be
an unlimited number of more solar systems outside
that, which they could begin upon afterwards. And
he warmed the hearts of Monopol and his friends by
condoling with them on the absence of any wits
or writers of the age at all worthy of such notice
as theirs, while congratulating them that there had
formerly been one or two whom their art might yet
improve and elevate by enlightened interpretation.
It was to be regretted, the royal speaker admitted,
that, in this land of mind and plenty, literature
alone was dead, except in the wonderful columns of
the daily newspapers. Yet there was compensation

in that—for the newspapers were there to tell them so. The excitement of the special correspondents, at this point, made it almost impossible to hear more, and the king-consort took the opportunity of passing rapidly to his peroration, which had for its theme the virtues and the graces of his Floriline. If she were not present, he said, he should tell her that she was the fairest woman and the most perfect queen who had ever graced the earth, (which, by the by, was not far from true) that he knew already that there never had been, or could be, such a wife, and, little as it became him to say so, that she had never exhibited her appreciation of mental and physical qualities better than when she chose him for a husband. (Thunders of applause.) Whatever she wished, he would do—for she was not a woman ever to wish him to do anything he didn't like. As she was present, he said— after ten minutes of this—that he could not, of course, tell it her now, but he would leave his life and reign to prove it. So when the king-consort, the Baron Osy de Ankworks, sat down upon a

M

garden seat exhausted, but smiling, it was generally
agreed that no better speech had ever been made,
and that at none of the recent Butter-Feasts, as
they were called, which were the most popular and
best reported form of entertainment of the day in
Tadt—not even at the feasts of the Cock-horse, or
principal magistrate of Kashburg—had it been
surpassed in eloquence, taste, and modesty. An
unobserved witness of his rival's triumph, Binko
literally writhed.

But the silver cloud began now to turn out its
black lining, and the terrible reverse of this pleasing
episode was as sudden as the lightning out of a blue
sky. For shortly after this the guests gradually
dispersed, and left Floriline and Osy alone in the
smiling cocoa-grounds.   Indeed they needed it;
for they were a bonnie and winsome pair, and had
their royal feelings like other people. The pretty
queen was so moved by her husband's praises of
her (and, indeed, he felt them,) and blushed so
becomingly, and looked so tempting, that it wasn't
in nature for the two not to wish for a little time

to themselves. And it must be confessed that Floriline, who had been accustomed to have her royal way in everything, did not intend to be baulked in this matter, but succeeded in finding a convenient moment to give the whole court its dismissal until the general dinner hour. It is re-corded that she did so in the simple words, "You needn't stay here, my friends, if you had rather not;" and the gracious sweetness of her manner robbed the order, as it was at once perceived to be, of all sense of abruptness. Everybody, indeed, of any breeding—and it is not to be supposed that there could be anybody there without it—felt at once that he or she *had* rather not. And so the newly-wedded lovers were alone for the first time.

There are not many sweeter or shyer moments in life than that, that the historian has to tell of, and these two were very much and very honestly in love with each other. And so the young queen's frank eyes sought Osy's, and his looked back into them as frankly, and I really believe that they both forgot altogether that there was such a thing as a

crown or a sceptre in the world. The listeners in the cruel bushes, and the listening fairies that hovered in the flower-drops—alas! that by the law of

AND SO THE YOUNG QUEEN'S FRANK EYES SOUGHT OSY'S, AND HIS LOOKED BACK INTO THEM AS FRANKLY.

their fairy being they could give the lovers no

warning then—heard very little said. Lovers do
not make love to each other in duets, even in
Tadt; yet the fairy-poet might have written down
their love-talk in some such words as these :

HE

" I love you as the sun loves the roses on the stem ;
And I will kiss you gently, as the south wind kisses them ;
And as they breathe their passion back, in hues and scents divine,
So, darling, shall your soft lips leave their answer upon mine."

SHE

" I love you as the flowers love the sunshine and the heat ;
Or as they love the winds that woo with wanton breath and sweet,
And as for lack of air and light they sicken, droop, and pine,
So, darling, does my heart stand still, nor beat apart from thine !"

THEY

" My love ! my love ! I find no words to say
The thoughts that all are crowding upon my lips to-day ;
But in the book of lovers do no newer names appear
Than sweetheart, love, and darling ! and that art thou, my dear !"

"Why are you so expensive, dear?" Osy said
after a pause.

"What, my own ? "

"Pensive I mean. I'm a little confused with all that speaking, and now being left alone with you. You look wonderfully thoughtful, almost" he added, playfully, "as if you were in the blues."

"That's it!" Floriline cried suddenly, as if the fairies had given some secret warning and something were tightening about her heart.

"What's what?" asked her husband, astonished.

"The blues! Binko's Blues! Oh, Osy, I'm always thinking about that terrible pirate, who has sworn vengeance on me and mine, and now you know that means you!"

"My dear child, what nonsense! I've heard all about the blackguard, but he can't hurt you now."

"He was what you call a blackguard, I'm afraid," said Floriline, thoughtfully. The bushes over the sea, towards which the two had now wandered, suddenly rustled. "What in the world is that?" exclaimed the young queen. "There is no wind."

"No, love. But some tree which once brushed your lips is jealous of me, and saying so. Don't think about such a fellow as Binko any more, dear.

You've got a husband now to take care of you, of rank and family almost as good as your own."

"Rank is rank nonsense," said the pretty queen, looking up at him. Whereupon he did what I should have done, and kissed her.

"You dear little Radical," said Osy after this had been accomplished. "Fancy a queen a Radical! The Osy family, as can easily be traced through the loss of the first and last letters of the old name, descend directly from Moses."

"And from the lovely way in which his clothes are made," muttered the concealed Odonto, "the youth is still in the business." [1]

"Love," said Osy after a pause.

"Darling," added Floriline after another.

"My wife," was the next remark.

"My husband," was the fourth.

And there were accompaniments all through. The lovers were now on the brink of the treacherous sea, hidden from all view from the ground above, and the black soul of Binko could bear to witness

[1] Both Osy and Odonto were men of considerable education in matters outside their own map.

all this no longer. "Drop it!" he exclaimed, with
a yell; and with a shrill note upon his whistle he
sprang out of his ambush followed by Odonto, and
the ready Blues appeared from the rocks as arranged,
in answer to the sound; while, with six oarsmen as

EXCEPT TWO STRAIGHT BLOWS INTO THE EYE WITH LEFT AND RIGHT
FROM OSY.

ready, the *Cockle-Shell* was on the beach. Nothing
was ever more neat or complete or rapid, and the
Muse of History folds her wings before the awful
event. Even as Binko had planned, so it was done.
No sound could be uttered except one cry of sharp

distress from Floriline, and no deed done except two straight blows into the eye with left and right· from Osy which laid the two first assailants (of whom Binko was not one) upon the ground, and then all was over. Seized from behind, and pinioned and gagged, the gallant Baron and king-consort could do no more; and Floriline's pretty mouth, so much more pleasantly engaged but a minute before, had to submit to this last degradation too. Only one ear heard her cry—that of her faithful maid Euchrisma, who, haunted by suspicions suggested to her by Jetoline, about the sounds she had heard in the bushes, had crept out to watch over her beloved mistress. She sprang forward—but what could she do? In a moment, moreover, the eye of Odonto was attracted by her agreeable form, and he saw his chance of his own share of simple recreation. The faithful maiden, as becomes a confidante, came but to share her mistress's fate, and could only exchange despairing glances with her. In another minute, without the knowledge or observation of any of the brilliant

court who were, even now, pledging the royal
couple in their respective drinks and ways, the
deed was done, and the sturdy strokes of the oarsmen were conveying the captives to the *Tonic Bark*,
which only too soon received them.   Such was the
tragic ending of Queen Floriline's wedding day.

CHAPTER VIII.

IT was the open sea; and but a few months later, after the close of the last chapter, the *Tonic Bark* was cleaving her way, with a stiff breeze and the prospect of some dirty weather, through the blue surf of the Prolific Ocean. The mighty waters of the Prolific occupy a large space indeed in the other Map, and in one part or another they wash the shores of nearly all the principal countries and continents which appear in it. Breaking at the base of the cocoa-grounds of Maravilla as we have seen them on poor Floriline's ill-starred wedding-day, and laving all the southern coast of Tadt,

they curl round the fair shores of Cimarosa in an
easterly direction, and in the west they provide,
where they meet with the estuaries of the great
rivers, noble sea-ports for the big empire of
Karamsin. But far away southwards, where for
unknown thousands of miles no land is to be found
but here and there some rugged and isolated reef
of rock, known only in the chart of the mariner,
the Prolific reaches its mightiest where it stretches
out to the settlements of Dollarosa, and yet far
again beyond that towards still newer and less-
known continents, inhabited chiefly, if not still
exclusively, by cannibals and Amazons in the
towns, by wolves and boa-constrictors in the
rural districts, and by mosquitoes and missionaries
in both. Sometimes these strange countries would
send strange ambassadors with pig-tails to the
civilised north, who would return with travellers'
tales instead, having dressed themselves in the
garments of Tadt or Cimarosa, and having much
to tell about the manners and customs of Kashburg,
and the other great northern cities. For, thanks

to the rapid development of electricity, and steam-balloons, and diving-bells, and other means of communication, intercourse between the north and the far south was increasing every year.

In all these wild latitudes Binko was at home. He had sate under the sparkling Bandanna till the over-ripe fruit dropped in clusters upon his head; he had watched the dodo and the mastodon encounter the grisly bear or the racoon on the banks of strange rivers choked with tropical plants —rivers whose sources were undiscovered, and their very mouths as yet unknown; he had smoked his pipe at the dinners of the cannibals, and though not himself partaking, he had kindly taught them how the various arts of northern cookery might be applied to the human form; he had chucked many a comely Amazon under her well helmeted chin; and he had written several octavo volumes of travel, as well he might, which had gone through several editions each, and brought him much profit, both in the Tadtite and Dollarosan markets, as he was the only man who had ever been known in that sense to make the most of two worlds. He was indeed a pirate and an author both, as others have been before him.

It was to one of the wildest and least civilised of the cannibal sea-ports of the far south that Binko proposed to carry Floriline. He was himself well known there; but except for him and his Blues, once, and only once, had a party of travellers from the northern continent landed in the port of Bangdemonium. They were missionaries, and at first not unkindly received, especially by the young Amazon part of the population, who had never seen a curate before. But a pestilence broke out in the district, which made the native food very bad eating, but, in consequence of their more careful personal habits, did not affect the missionaries. After a time, therefore, the king and the royal family had really no choice but to cook them, which they did with much regret, all but one. The visitors had taught the poor savages some of the best habits of the north; so one was kept alive

to act as chaplain, and to say grace before meat.
It was the existence of this Tadtite missionary
which determined Binko's plan. He altered his
views about Osy after much conference with
Odonto, and on the voyage, instead of ill-treating,
he fattened him. It was the wicked purpose of
Binko, on reaching Bangdemonium, to sell the
king-consort to the royal cook, from whom he
knew that he could realise a better price for him
than in any other quarter, the cook being also
a retail dealer, and Osy of the most refined and
tender qualities. Then he proposed to give to
Floriline certain proof of her husband's death, con-
cealing the painful circumstances ; and, after a
reasonable time he would marry the widow, after
overcoming any scruples which she might entertain,
the missionary chaplain performing the ceremony
according to all the rites of the Tadtite Church,
so that there could be no mistake at all about it.
Then, as the husband of Floriline, he would return
in triumph to Tadt and reign happily ever after. It
seemed to Binko quite a providential arrangement,

cook, court, missionary, and all ; for his influence
with the reigning family and with the population
of Bangdemonium was entire, and he knew that he
might rely upon their friendship even under so
severe a strain as the peculiarly attractive and
digestible appearance of Floriline herself. Such
was the pirate's scheme, and the purpose of the
rest of my history is to show what became of it.

CHAPTER IX.

IT was noticeable that, at the point which this history has reached, there were ominous signs of discontent among the crew of the *Tonic Bark*. They had taken to holding clandestine meetings on the bowsprit or in the binnacle, to shirking work in a manner quite new among the members of that celebrated band, and to mysterious discussions in corners like those which took place in the public-houses on the night before the abduction of Queen Floriline. For it is a fact that this abduction, and all that followed it, created something very like a revolution in the course of life on board

N

the *Bark.* The presence of two petticoats among
the Blues, in the youngest and most attractive form
which that destructive garment can assume, caused
a considerable excitement among the more in-
flammable members of the band, which became
dangerous as soon as it was known that Floriline
and her maid were to take all their meals in the
captain's private room, instead of conforming to the
rules of the ship and sitting down regularly at the
table-d'hôte. The crew after some consultation sent
a round-robin to Binko upon the subject, but he
received it very badly and with an outburst of
fury, headmasting the unlucky bearer of the
message for two nights and a day without food,
after first knocking him about a good deal over the
head and shoulders with his inseparable stick ; and
this though the poor man had no more to do with it
than any of the others who signed the round-robin,
but was chosen by ballot to carry it, and had even
taken the precaution to bring a flag of truce with
him. Binko's neglect of the laws of courtesy, which
governed all respectable pirates in the world of the

other Map, added fuel to the flame which was now smouldering sullenly in the breasts of the band. The captain's attentions to Floriline meanwhile were of the most devoted and insidious nature; he made himself agreeable to her in every possible way, watching over her diet with unceasing personal attention, and pampered her with a special dish of lentils prepared after the fashions of the delicious continent of Revalenta Dubarrica, and washed down by juices of the fragrant lime-tree. He exhausted his brain in providing her with amusements calculated to while away the long hours of the day. He put up old fishing-nets across the deck for her and Euchrisma to knock balls over, himself and the captive baron joining in the sport, regardless of the manner in which they got in the way of the sailors at their work, and paying no heed to the muttered execrations in which an acute observer would have detected the signs of a rising storm. Any service that it was in his power to give her, he was wont playfully to say as he struck the ball to her across the net, he was sure that she

wished to return ; and it was the deuce (here it must
be admitted that he spoke rather coarsely) if she had
not got the advantage. He also frequently alluded
to crossing the line. In after times Floriline remembered these expressions, and founded upon
them a game which became very^ popular with the
youth of Tadt, and quite superseded that which
had so long commemorated her ancestor Aunt
Sally. When in a moment of admiration for her
sunny beauty Binko declared that he should
scarcely give her half thirty, so girlish did she
look, her ready wit at once utilised the expression
for the purposes of the game. Such was the
historic origin of a famous sport.

In the calm summer evenings the enamoured
pirate loved to lie at Floriline's feet, singing her
light and humorous songs upon the ojnab,* an instrument much in use for ditties of the kind,
and striking it with his head and knee and
knuckles indiscriminately, to produce continuous
melody. If it be asked how the captive queen
received these attentions, it must be admitted in

answer that she enjoyed them exceedingly, and
with all the keen sense of fun which never

BINKO PLAYING THE OJNAB.

abandoned her even in her present extremity.   It
was a delight to her to watch the contortions of
the great little man in the tall black hat, and the

wonderful faces that he made whilst he twisted his
features into what he considered irresistible forms
of expression, and laid persevering siege to her
heart. In confidential moments she allowed him
to point out to her how easily her marriage with
the Baron Osy de Ankworks might be dissolved, and
even discussed the question with him at times quite
seriously, and as one who feels that she may have
made a mistake. For the truth is that the first
she-oyster at the bottom of that original Tadtite
pond had handed down her inherent spirit of
mischief to her latest descendant, through all
structural changes and evolutions, in unimpaired
completeness; and I am not sure that Queen
Floriline was not a very decided little flirt. Besides
that, of course, she had in view the serious purpose of blinding the eyes of her dangerous admirer,
and seizing upon the first opportunity of effecting
her escape at all costs. She confided her schemes
to Osy and Euchrisma, who fully understood that
the best thing they had to do was to fall in with
them; and the baron, whom Binko treated in the

most liberal and friendly manner with the diabolical object I have already described, assumed with great effect the airs and appearance of a disappointed and dejected lover, dropping altogether the authority of a husband, which, indeed, was the one thing which the pirate declined to allow him to exercise in any way. Binko was in the seventh heaven of triumph. And it would have been delightful to any one who might have been there, to watch Floriline's laughing imitations of him when she was alone with Osy and Euchrisma.

Meanwhile a perilous enemy to Binko's peace was on the watch on board. For some time, from various incidental circumstances, the Lieutenant Odonto had been suspicious of Binko's real intentions as to the restoration of the Ivory Kingdom to him, its original owner. In his quiet and sententious way he had let fall various remarks calculated to bring out the truth from the captain; and at last one day he succeeded in hiding himself behind a pile of pirated manuscripts, and overhearing one of the conversations which took place between Floriline and Binko in one of the latter's most unguarded moments, when the pretty queen was turning his head with flattery, and drawing him on. He warned her who Odonto really was and what were his designs, and on her professing terror he told her how useful he found the ex-king in the capacity of lieutenant, through the

ODONTO LISTENING BEHIND MANUSCRIPTS.

personal motives which secured his active fidelity. He proceeded to laugh at the unhappy man's blind confidence, and assured Floriline that if he ever should have her interests to look after, she might feel very sure indeed that the Ivory Kingdom would never cease to be a jewel of the Tadtite crown. Odonto heard all, and thought more. In a moment it occurred to him that if he could find the opportunity of driving a bargain with Floriline on his own account, he might secure the restoration of the Ivory Kingdom to himself by undertaking to replace Floriline on the throne of Tadt with the aid of the disaffected spirits of the band, who were growing more and more weary of Binko's ways and habits, and were now on the verge of mutiny. Moreover, he would further influence Floriline by bestowing his hand and heart upon her favourite Euchrisma, and seating her by his side in the famous inclined chair. So it was that at the time when the dirty weather described at the beginning of the last chapter began to grow threatening, the *Bark* being now but within a few days' sail of Bangdemonium, all these various schemes were simmering in the various heads of the travellers, and everything, figuratively and literally, was ripe for a squall.

CHAPTER X.

"THIS is a pretty state of things, upon my word!" gruffly exclaimed Indigo the Blue as he sate upon the poop, round which several of the band were collected on that threatening morning, as the *Bark* coursed through the southern seas before the rising wind. "To bring a brace of petticoats aboard ship, and give us a heap of extra work to do!"

"The captain's going it," said Verditer in a lighter blue tone than the other.

"Work!" added one Ultramarine in a voice of extreme disgust. "And we the working-classes? It isn't to be expected of us."

" It's a full fortnight since our wages were raised," said Cobalt.

" And a month since our hours were shortened," growled Indigo.

" I can't stand that old Binko any longer," cried the third.

" He bullies his Blues till they're blacks and blues," added another of the discontented. " Look where he fetched me across the shoulders with that old stick of his last night, because I didn't get up the lady's maid's beef-tea in time !"

" Yah ! yah ! beef-tea !" cried an old salt with a tumbler of grog before him. " These class-comforts is disgusting things, and the way these women is pampered with them is past bearing. I've known one as rubbed a whole tallow candle on her nose at one time. What are we a-going to do about it, mates ?" he added excitedly, as his thoughts became too much for him.

" It's organise we must," Indigo answered. " There's nothing like organising to set things straight when they go crooked."

"The captain wants a deal of organising when he's had his nightcap, then," quickly observed Odonto, who had joined the group unnoticed.

"The lieutenant, by Jingo!" exclaimed Indigo, jumping to his feet, with an instinctive appeal to the war god of the Tadtites, which found a response at once in the heart of every man present. They began to brandish their cutlasses with angry gestures, and to cast hostile glances upon the intruder.

"Are you going to split, lieutenant?" said Ultramarine in a low tone.

"I am," replied Odonto.

"Ha!"

"A drink, if you will give me one," the lieutenant said composedly, as he sate down amongst the men. And with a relieved laugh a messmate handed him the generous liquor, of which he drained a long draught in silence before he spoke again. The men watched him with anxiety.

"Thank you," were the first words he said. "I'm better; now to business. Before you get rid of the old captain, you know, my men, you must

decide upon your new one." The others looked
at him with astonishment.

" You don't mean to say that you'll go in with
us, lieutenant ? " exclaimed Indigo. " You and
the captain are as thick as thieves."

" He's a spy ; that's what he is ! " muttered the
old salt. " Better pitch un overboard and make
no bones about it."

The suggestion was received with so many signs
of approval that the lieutenant felt no time was
to be lost.

" Men of the *Tonic Bark!* " he at once began,
with a manly quiver in his voice, " is it possible
that you can have so mistaken your lieutenant ?
Is it possible that you have not seen through
appearances, and discovered the fatherly interest
which I take in your well-being ? "

" You've walloped us with the rope's end often
enough," said Cobalt practically.

" That was interest," answered Odonto. " Spare
the rope and spoil the pirate, is a maxim which
you all know well."

"We haven't been much spoiled aboard this, then, at that rate," remarked the gentleman who had complained of his shoulders, rubbing them. "When the captain leaves off, you have a way of beginning."

"Discipline is good for all of us, and the captain has not unfrequently struck me. I bear him no grudge for that, my dear friends, for I feel that it has made a man of me, and a man not disposed to put up with any more nonsense. Boys," added Odonto, looking round on the crew, "what is it that the captain has been promising all of you when he returns to Tadt from this expedition?"

A chorus of the men interrupted him. Binko had been lavish of promises. It was an understood thing that this was their last piratical cruise, upon which they were to return in triumph and respectability to seat Binko on the throne with Floriline, and to divide all the principal offices and emoluments in the kingdom between them. To the old salt, for instance, were to be confided the

seals of First Secretary at Land because he had lived
all his life on the sea; and when on one occasion he
had made himself particularly disagreeable about
arrears of wages, Binko had gone so far as to make
out his patent in due form under his own royal
seal, and to provide that the salary should count
from the date of the patent as soon as he entered
upon his duties. Similar arrangements and engage-
ments had been made with every member of the
crew, and it was their hope that something might
come of them which so far had staved off the crisis,
which the growing discontent caused by the presence of the captives on board and the consequent
upset of all their ways of life, must otherwise have
brought about by this time. Binko's behaviour
throughout the cruise had nearly fanned into a flame
the embers of hatred which were always smouldering round that most unpopular man, and more
than once it had occurred to the crew that their
best plan after all might be to secure the persons
of Binko and his lieutenant and dispose of them
quickly, and then to convey Floriline and Osy

safely back to Tadt, and bring about a monarchical
restoration on condition of being pardoned all round
and received into favour at court, which the queen
and king-consort could hardly refuse them. Even
if they could not expect to be made ministers of
the crown, they felt instinctively that it might be
safer and wiser to stipulate for and to accept a
good deal less than that from sovereigns on whom
they all knew that they might rely, than to place
any further confidence in the word of Binko. But
for the absence of any leading mind among them
it is probable that these ideas would have borne
fruit by this time, during the months for which the
Tonic Bark had been speeding over the Prolific
Seas. But it was just this absence of a leader
which had been so far fatal to any effective
combination ; and had not the pirate chief been so
entirely absorbed in his admiration for Floriline
and his devotion to the new game of net-and-ball,
which seemed to have the property of entirely
monopolising the mind attracted to it, he could
scarcely have failed to have had his suspicions

awaked to the plots and secret meetings which were going on, and to have provided carefully and effectually against any upset of his plans. A very close examination of the archives of Kashburg, and study of state-papers not previously at the historian's disposal, have enabled me to show, with much more clearness than has hitherto been possible, the various motives and machinations which were at work at this grave crisis of Tadtite history. On springs of conduct so petty and selfish, and on circumstances apparently so minute and trivial, does the fate of dynasties in truth depend.

The presence and help of Odonto was exactly what the men required, as he very quickly proved to them. Undistracted by the burning love which had mastered the soul of Binko, and only paying agreeable attentions to the pretty Euchrisma which gratified without absorbing either of them, he did not find himself invited to join in the game of net-and-ball, except very occasionally, when one of the four was tired (which was scarcely ever), and

o

had not therefore grown interested in it to the point of forgetfulness. He was indeed very wide-awake throughout the voyage, and followed up the opportunity he had found of overhearing Binko and Floriline from behind the manuscripts, by a close though felonious examination of the pirate's papers. Armed with the knowledge so obtained of Binko's secret plans, and oppressed—being himself a good man—by the depth of depravity which he thereby discovered in his captain, he presented himself before the gathering of Blues as described at the beginning of this chapter, and was soon in possession of their entire confidence. For he was able to assure them that Binko was deceiving them all. His patent of First Secretary at Land was not worth the paper it was written upon. He had no intention whatever of rewarding any of them, or indeed of taking any of them home. His plans, at the outset diabolical, had matured in his mind till no epithet could describe them. *It was his intention to dispose of the whole crew to the Bangdemonians, on touching port, for articles of food, along with the Baron Osy*, and, availing himself of his influence with the savage potentate, to replace them by a select body of Amazons instructed in navigation, who would accompany himself and Floriline home. Upon their arrival the Amazons would appear at the Royal Theatre, in a play especially written for them by the Brothers Pinaphor, introduced in an elegy by Lilliflop, and afterwards go round the country under careful management, and return to their native continent in the possession of immense wealth. They would all be beautiful, and that they knew nothing at all about acting would be an advantage rather than otherwise in the eyes of the Tadtites, who did not care for meretricious attractions.

Terrible was the wrath of Binko's Blues when Odonto revealed the plan. Their first instinct was to fly upon Binko, then engaged at net-and-ball with Queen Floriline at the other end of the ship, and tear him limb from limb. But Odonto pointed out that they had plenty of time to do things quietly and in order, and to indulge in the pleasure of a slower revenge. "Let us wound him in all his most cherished feelings," he said ; and the sentiment was much approved. "Let us make him unloose his purse-strings—for he has untold gold on board, though he pretends to be without ready-money— and force him to pay up, coin by coin. We will strike, my oppressed brothers !" cried Odonto, waxing eloquent. (Hear, hear.) "If coals and meat can rise, as he always tells us when we ask for more money, why so can we and wages." (Applause.) "But let us be in order when we hold a meeting, and be within our rights. Who'll move a resolution ?"

"I will—I will—I will," exclaimed many Blues.

"One at a time," said a voice from the crowd.

"Nonsense ! at meetings everybody speaks at once," said another. "Indigo, Indigo !" And clearing his throat, Indigo began, "I move that we make Binko change his note." "Nobody would give him change for a sixpence," said the voice from the crowd.

"Hear, hear," from some. "Sit down!" from others. "Meetings don't stand on forms!" "They do!" cried one on a bench, "and smash them if necessary." "Is this a land of freedom?" cried the indignant Indigo.

"No! it's a water of freedom."

"Turn him out! Knock him down!"

"Hear, hear." And, whoever he was, he was knocked down, and turned out. There is no need to enter at further length into the proceedings of the meeting, which was as all earnest meetings are. Odonto was accepted as leader. The strike was unanimously carried, and it was agreed to demand that all wages on board should be raised one-third : that working hours for the future should be from twelve to four, but that from one to three the men should all knock off for dinner, and that more labour than that should be capital. Odonto was to give the signal for the strike, in a manner agreed upon that very afternoon, as soon as Binko began to bluster and grow abusive to the men, as was his invariable custom after lunch. The first step in

the mutiny successfully taken, it was to be reserved for further consideration what should
be done next, and by what steps the dis-
comfiture and punishment of Binko should be
completely carried out. The meeting dispersed
well-satisfied, and among that band of hardy sailors
there was none to take note of the gathering
sough and moan of the wind, of the black pile of
clouds rising up mountains high all round
them, of the blacker waters seething sullenly
under like a witch's cauldron, and of the uncom-
fortably increasing motion of the vessel, far from
all sight of land.

CHAPTER XI.

FLORILINE, playing net-and-ball at the other end of the vessel, began to feel the motion very much. Her best twisted services showed signs of pitching outside the line, and the ship pitched too. Indeed she pitched tremendously. The favourable weather which had attended the pirate's venture ever since the start had been so uniformly delightful that it had gone a long way to reconcile the young queen to the situation. With plenty to eat and drink, with the pirate's astonishing love-making to amuse her, with her husband and her favourite maid at her elbow, and with the happy

confidence of youth and bounding health to
convince her that all would come right in the end
—the sweet young queen was really enjoying her
strange outing in spite of fate. It was so
pleasant to be rid of all the cares and pomps of
state, which considerably oppressed her young spirits
at times, and to know that the pages of the
Palace Circular must be blank about her every
morning, or confine themselves to guesses as to
the whereabouts of the *Tonic Bark*, which all
the Tadtite fleet were following in vain, in all
directions except the right one. It is true that
some days had passed before any of it was ready
to follow at all. With nobody to chronicle what
she ate and where she ate it; to say exactly whom
she called on and who called upon her; with no
ladies in waiting always on the premises, and no
ministers to worry her with business; without a
single paper to sign or letter to answer; with
nothing to read but old numbers of the *Pirate's
Journal* and the *Dollarosan Privateer;* and,
above all, without the remotest chance of having

to listen to the lectures, public or private, of the
Hair-Professor Shpex, the sweet Floriline was
really happy up to the moment which our history
has reached. For at night-time upon her silky
pillow, and in the land of dreams, when with the
pretty mouth ever so slightly parted over the
ivory teeth which Floriline the Fragrant preserved
in miraculous whiteness, she looked too pretty for
anything—there can be little doubt that she had
a full deputation of her old friends the fairies
with her. Her lips sometimes moved in her sleep
as she held conferences with them, so close and real
as to make her rub her eyes when she woke, and
look round in wonder and disappointment for the
dainty presences which had hovered about her but
the moment before. But when they visited her
again the next night and the next, and never failed
to repeat their confident assurance of safety and
defence, she became quietly convinced of the
reality of her midnight visitors, and knew that
it was only part of the law of their fairy-being
that she could only see and speak with them with

the eye and voice of sleep, when the finer spirit within her was free to make holiday for a time, and to disport itself in the regions which by day are only tenanted by the kindred spirits which have no bodies to bother them, or, if they ever had, have succeeded in getting rid of them. So convinced did Floriline become of this during that eventful voyage, that all that Shpex could say and prove in the after-years about brain-matter and unconscious cerebration could never undo the mischief which those months had done to her mind. The queen never would have anything more to do with metaphysics, and never would look at the *Present Sentry*. She said—and it caused a great sensation—that those things were all very well for people who had nothing to do, except to make themselves and everybody else miserable. It was shortly after that declaration that Shpex retired into an Asylum for Thinkers which the state had at last to provide for that body, when they outgrew the bounds of all possible magazines too entirely to be able to provide for themselves : and he was heard

of no more on this side of the Indefinite. The
Sage-green Committee was thereupon dissolved—in
tears. On the night before the occurrences now
being related took place on board the *Bark*, the
sleeping queen was surprised by a sudden fairy
whisper. "Floriline, Floriline, don't forget the
ring and its use, for the time is coming when you
will need it." With the words ringing in her ear
Floriline awoke, and she was thinking what they
might mean when the rising of the water
interrupted her game of net-and-ball. For the seas
were rising round the *Tonic Bark* with increasing
fury, and the views of Queen Floriline as to the
pleasures of an abduction began to be very sensibly
modified. Binko, of course, as would naturally be
the case with a pirate, revelled in the discord of the
elements and the roar of the waters, and proceeded
to indulge in language which it would be beneath
the dignity of history to repeat. The gallant Osy,
long accustomed to the sea in the course of his
weekly passages to his barony of Ankworks and
back, took the change of weather at first quietly

enough, though his experienced eye watched the
black horizon with increasing anxiety. But the
queen and her faithful attendant began to feel far
from well, and their faces betrayed uneasiness of a
less far-seeing but more pressing kind.

"What swell is there so heavy," exclaimed the
pirate captain as he proudly trod the deck of the
bark, and smoothed the wrinkles from his frock-
coat with signs of self-approval, "as a swell at
sea?"

"The fellow's fine airs are very offensive,"
whispered Osy to Floriline, whom he was trying to
reassure.

"They are not so offensive as his cors-airs,
dear," murmured the young queen. I do not
think that I have yet mentioned that by the
common law of Tadt everybody was obliged to
make puns in conversation; and even in times
of extremity it was understood that the law
was supreme. Indeed they were apt to develop
the latent national tendency; and the excited
Binko proceeded with an appeal to the waves.

"Ha, ha!" he exclaimed, "see how like an advertising Dollarosan publisher my gallant bark is, puffing her pirate sail!"

"The pirate's ale will be a bitter bier ere long," said Osy, contemplating the weather. "Yet cheer up, my Floriline! Wherever we wander, the salt spray will always remind us of (f) oam."

"Give me my salts, pray," was the unsteady reply.

"Angel, suffer me!" exclaimed the baron, offering a richly-jewelled salts-cellar.

"I will," the queen whispered. "I suffer a good deal at sea."

"There is water in your eyes, my queen!" exclaimed the pirate.

"There is indeed," said Floriline, "and nothing else."

"I meant not that," answered Binko. "I mean that you are weeping. Let me, too, drop the private-tear for a moment, and point out to you the beauties of the scene. Be not alarmed, my sovereign! See how gallantly we speed before the wind! See how my bark is riding the white horses of the sea——"

"It is a rider to a very disagreeable motion," interrupted the pretty Euchrisma, who could command her feelings no longer. "For mercy's sake let me get to my berth, or it will be the death of me! The lady's maid is bound to be ill the first, and I cannot stand it."

She looked as if she could not; for even as she spoke she fell rather than walked down the companion-ladder kept for her use as the queen's companion (her majesty only used the principal stair-case), and for the time was seen no more.

.　　.　　.　　.　　.

The strife of the elements was at its height: and, by the strange perversion of ideas to which the strongest of men are liable at moments, Binko, excited to a kind of frenzy by the storm, was pressing his untimely suit on Floriline. No one was near them. The gallant Osy, who, in all his experiences of the strip of sea which separated Tadt from the barony of Ankworks, had never met with anything at all resembling the Prolific in its accesses of rage, had himself, though not without a struggle that was worthy of him, succumbed for a time to the influences which had subdued the spirit of Euchrisma, and detecting the passage of a green shade over his complexion, and feeling that there are moments when only in solitude can there be true dignity, like her had sought the seclusion of his berth. As for the crew—strange indeed at such a time—few of them were to be seen anywhere, except that here and there two or three would occasionally come together, cast ominous looks upon the pirate-chief, and converse in low whispers which the roar of the ocean effectually drowned. Entirely carried away by his feelings, Binko failed to remark anything unusual amongst the men, or to see that the *Tonic Bark*, practically left to her own devices, was speeding headlong over the boiling surf of the Prolific without the guide of compass or rudder.

"A few more days of this, my queen, and we

shall drive straight into the port of Bangdemonium !" he cried out to her who alone shared his
watch upon deck. "This squall but takes us
straight upon the right course, and then you shall
know——"

"Know I shall not," said the queen decisively.
She never looked so beautiful as she did at this
moment. The royal spirit of the girl had entirely
subdued in her all sense of weakness as the sense
of danger rose; and she looked a sea-queen to
the manner born. Her soft long hair was tossing
loose about her back; her eyes had a light like
opals and diamonds in them, and the rich blood
which flushed into her cheek seemed to make them
flash the more. The very figure seemed to have
gained fresh height and dignity from the occasion,
as the proud head curved backwards while with
her right arm she steadied herself against the
vessel's side, and with a new scorn in her eyes
she looked defiance on her detested lover. The fairy-
whisper of the night before seemed to have given
her a strange sense of secure protection ; and, like

the true woman that she was, in the danger which she felt all round them, she rose above pretence.

"Leave me," she said, "and begone!"

"What?" Binko almost screamed. "What? When I love you?"

"Love me—you!" she answered, with a withering scorn. "Why, man, we are all driving straight to destruction, and do you think that a queen will palter or talk nonsense at such a time as this? Love me, you wretch! How dare you?"

"What?" the pirate quite screamed, this time, upon a sharper note. "I tell you I love and adore you! A cat doesn't love cream better! A grouse doesn't love the heather better! A lawyer doesn't love a fee better! Those cruel charms of yours are more deeply branded in my whirling brain, than my last consignment of contraband sherry! My passion boils my blood and fries my soul, my—my—" And he shouted more and more, and the waters rose higher and higher.

"That's right!" said Floriline, with infinite contempt. "Keep up the bawl, do, though our game

P

is over. There isn't much of you, little man ; but
what there is certainly makes noise enough for
two.   You can't be accused of singing small,
whatever you look."

"Small !" he echoed.   "If you could only see
my heart—if you could only read my love ! I
love you so that I could eat you like a Bang-
demonian, much as you would disagree with me
and the idea !"

"A heavy dinner," she said, in the same un-
changing tone ; "but I really believe you are not
without the sauce to do it.   I shouldn't digest
so easily, my good pirate !"

"What, what !" cried Binko again, as the scorn
in the queen's voice became too much for him.
"Digest, indeed !   I'll tell you what it is then.
Your Osy shall die just now, and before your eyes."

"Pooh !" said the queen.   It is incredible :
but all she said was " Pooh."

"You don't believe me !" shrieked Binko.
": Then it shall be worse.   I keep a terrible minion
concealed upon this bark, by name Euxesis, or the

Easy Shaver! Once let him prepare his deadly weapons at my bidding, and—" he hissed into the queen's ear—"he will take off all the baron's skin, and leave the hair!"

"Don't!" said Floriline, in a mocking tone of entreaty; for she saw the coming fate in the whirl of waters, and her courage rose high at the prospect of so wild a release. "Don't! He is—" and the spirit of mischief took possession of her again, as, at a crisis, it will—"he is such a darling!"

"Hang him!" yelled the jealous pirate.

"I sha'n't," she answered. "I simply worship him—bless him!" What might have followed it is difficult to say; for the infuriated Binko sprang forward to seize his captive in his arms, while she drew back in grand defiance.

"Touch me, if you dare—you ugly little man!" she said.

Even Binko shrank for a second from the look in her eyes, and that second was enough to allow the Baron Osy, himself again at the proper

moment, as all true lovers are, to stand like a rock
between them, and to throw Binko to the other

"TOUCH ME, IF YOU DARE—YOU UGLY LITTLE MAN!" SHE SAID.

side of the deck with one arm, while with the
other he encircled the form of Floriline.

"My love!" she cried.

"My own!" he answered. "Courage! I see land, or something like it. Jump into the sea with me, and don't fear."

"How should I fear drowning," she said, clinging closer to his arm, "with such a life-preserver as this round my waist?"

Binko literally yelled. "Up, Blues, and at them!" he cried, sounding a shrill dog-whistle, which out-whistled the wind as he applied it to his teeth. Then first he began to realise the situation, for no Blues were there. "Where are you, Blues?" he added. "Confound it, there's nobody steering!"

There was not. Only the placid figure of Odonto quietly faced the enraged captain, and one or two other Blues, whose sea-legs were affected by nothing, lounged quietly on deck.

"Here we are," said Odonto.

"Seize them!—arrest them!—drown them!" screamed Binko, while Floriline and Osy, seeing the state of affairs, deferred their header.

"The work doesn't suit our book, captain," said Indigo..

"And we sha'n't stir a step," added Verditer.

"Unless we're paid for it," remarked Cobalt, decisively.

"Steps by purchase are abolished," shouted Binko. "At him, and strike!"

"Precisely what we mean to do," said Odonto, as the others gathered about him.

"This is conspiracy!" exclaimed the pirate.

"No; trades-union," said the old salt entering.

"What! You're the steersman?"

"Precisely. The spokes-man from the wheel."

"Go and steer!" commanded Binko, beside himself with fury.

"I sha'n't. The ship may steer herself, boys, eh?"

"Hear, hear!" said Odonto. "The ship of state often does."

"Is my hated enemy to be saved in this way?" cried the baffled pirate, foaming at the mouth in a way which really made him pitiable to look at. "Shiver my timbers!"

The ancient nautical exclamation might have been a prayer, so suddenly was it answered. With one deafening crash fore and aft, in the middle of a pitchy blackness and the roar of waters, the *Tonic Bark* grounded suddenly upon a rock. " Hang it ! they are shivered !" added the captain, helplessly.

In a moment all was confusion. " Where are we ?" " Look out !" " What is it ?" " All hands !" " Right tack !" " Left tack !" " The reef—the reef !" " Confusion !"

" Yes, indeed," exclaimed Binko, his round yet active figure in the centre of the scene. " That's what your strikes lead to, and what comes of example. The ship herself has struck now, and be hanged to you !"

It was even so. A cry of rising voices, and the upturning of lifted hands; a swirl of water and a crash of beams; figures fighting and struggling in the furious sea, and huge white rocks towering majestically out of its boiling depths—and breaking up in one supreme moment the *Tonic · Bark* went down like a lead-line into a fathomless grave. She had grounded on a terrible rock too well known in those latitudes. The crew were shipwrecked on the Chloral Reef.

CHAPTER XII.

THE CHLORAL REEF.

ALL the elements of discomfort are present at a shipwreck, especially the water. There was a large quantity of that about upon this occasion; even more than upon most, for the Prolific Ocean is notoriously upon an unusual scale. And it seethed and roared like a huge witch's cauldron round the dangerous crystals of the Chloral Reef.

It was a reef well known in the charts of the mariners, and much too well known to be trusted. It was a strange oasis of white rock in the middle of that mighty sea, at some days' sail from the

port of Bangdemonium. It was compounded
entirely of rock crystals not soluble in salt water ;
otherwise of course it would have disappeared
long ago. The crystals were of different lustre
and sizes, and consisted of different amounts of
grains. And there were wild whispers abroad
about the strange mysteries of the wondrous rock,
which was reported to be a favourite haunt for
the supernatural members of the spirit-world, as
much the home of magic shapes and fancies as
Prospero's enchanted island. One especial property
was attributed to the Reef, of whose origin no
clear account could be given. *No mortal that had
ever been cast away upon it had ever returned
awake.* Few there were that had ever returned
at all, and many the bones left mouldering among
the crystals, in eternal sleep. Those daring
explorers who had deliberately and of purpose
trusted themselves upon the rock, had sometimes
been seen upon fine days to lose themselves more
and more among the snowy crystals, which had
quite an alluring and tranquillising effect upon

many, and stumbling at last between those which contained the greatest number of grains, to be seen of man no more. Those who from time to time were rescued by some passing vessel which had the presence of mind not to do more than touch at the Reef, came back to the world under the singular condition mentioned; and, though occasionally pinched or pricked into a momentary state of stupid half-consciousness, invariably relapsed into a hopeless lethargy. They moved about as in a drugged state among men, unable to give any intelligible account of their sensations, or of what had befallen them upon the Reef, and it was difficult for their friends to know what to do with them. Bangdemonium being the nearest port, and its king and inhabitants being, as far as is consistent with cannibalism, of a gentle and charitable disposition, quite a colony of these unhappy people had been established in a quiet quarter of the town, who under the name of the Hebetites had gradually married and intermarried, and transmitted their mysterious peculiarity to

their descendants. As they were never long-lived,
however, and never increased in numbers, they were
not what it was once feared they might be, a danger
to the State. When that fear first arose, the State
naturally proposed that they should be eaten ; but
as the necessary medical examination by the Court
insurance-officer proved that they were not wholesome for the purpose, and as the destruction of
human life in any other way was strictly forbidden
in Bangdemonium, the quarter was finally railed
round and thrown open for exhibition upon a
certain payment, and half-price on Saturdays. It
may be added that at one time tidings of the
Blue Rosette Bill reached Bangdemonium in a
roundabout way, through some of the various
embassies, and the king, always anxious for the
last civilised improvements, talked with his
ministers about introducing it. But a careful
inquiry by the Court insurance-officer having
clearly established that the denial of all consoling
drinks to the population must result in a dangerous
tendency to the increase of Hebetism, the idea

was promptly abandoned. For the early Hebetites had brought away pieces of the crystals with them, and it was believed they were still used for nefarious purposes in the quarter.

Upon this terrible and mysterious reef had Floriline and her fortunes foundered. There must have been some strange powers watching in the air, for hardly had the wicked bark gone to pieces for ever upon the crystal peaks, when the sky began to clear and the sea to subside, and the ill-starred crew, with the help of binnacles, mizens, bowsprits, booms, and bunks, or anything they could lay their hands on from the wreck, to struggle on to the rocky shelf of the Reef, which formed a picturesque platform of considerable extent, dotted with crystal prominences, at the height of some feet above the water. One figure might first have been seen to emerge and to scramble to a foot-hold, hurting its fingers a good deal in the process, but uttering no complaint. It was the figure of a depressed and middle-aged man, about whom everything was dripping except his philo-

sophy, which remained as dry as ever. It
was indeed the dethroned king and lieutenant,
Odonto, who vaguely looked about him when he
had gained the flat. There were strange rustlings
and whispers in the air above him, as of a kind

ONE FIGURE MIGHT FIRST HAVE BEEN SEEN TO EMERGE.

of suppressed laughter, and the magical spirit of the
place descending upon him, he began after a time
to talk, as those who came under its influence did,
in a confused and prosaic sort of verse, which was
ever and again the form of language enforced
upon those who were landed on the mystic Reef.

He spoke to himself, for the simple reason that there was nobody else to speak to ; but audibly, and thus :

" The worst of being shipwrecked is, you get, while in the water, so extremely wet ; and the deserted soul existence loathes, when nothing sticks to him except his clothes. Oh Fate, Oh Fortune, why are you so vexed with me ? what do you mean, I wonder, to do next with me ?

" Dear me ! " he proceeded, " I have never been accustomed to talk in poetry. Indeed, I never liked it, and have been a matter-of-fact person all my life. What's that, I wonder ? " said he with a start, distinctly feeling something he could not see pinch him in the calf, and at the same time a kind of heavy invisible hand laid for a moment upon his eyes, leaving a sudden and rather pleasant sense of sleepiness behind it, which made the gallant lieutenant feel rather more stupid than usual, and was even slightly suggestive of drink. He sate upon a little crystal knoll but a few grains in weight, and proceeded

with his soliloquy, looking about him with a dull
sort of curiosity at the white rocks around.

" I've not an-ocean what this place may be, but
must find out, because I came to sea ; so let me
think my last misfortunes o'er : a capfull o' wind
upset us on the shore—"

At this point, I grieve to say, somebody else
was heard to make a very strong remark about
"that cap's-ize." Odonto looked sleepily up
at the remarker, and with some difficulty recognised Binko in the limp and washed-out figure
before him. The shapely frock-coat clung with
a new and unbecoming tightness to the circular
form ; and from the effect of sudden immersion in
an unusual element, the fiery nose pronounced
itself more strongly than ever. But the burning
tropical sun, which was now bursting out in royal
splendour after the storm, proceeded to dry the
captain. As he began to dry he began to miss his
drink, and glowered furiously at Odonto. He
abused the cap's-ize again. Odonto only looked
at him sleepily and yawned. " I've heard that

joke somewhere before," he said. " That doesn't
matter in our trade," growled Binko. " I'm a
pirate, and I adapted it. Look here, lieutenant,"
he added, sharply, " where are we ? "

" I don't know," said Odonto, " and I don't care.
But whatever ' here ' may mean, how did you get
here ? "

" On a broken mast," answered the captain.
" I took a promenade on the Spar. I repeat,
where are we ? You're my lieutenant, and you've
got to know."

" However, I don't," yawned the other. " All
I do know is, that there's something in the air."

" Of course, ozone," said Binko, promptly.
Everybody in Tadt was expected to talk about
science, whether it bored him or not. But
Odonto was not in a scientific humour, and, much
to his chief's astonishment, who had never heard
him quote poetry before, he fell altogether under
the spirit of the place, and in sentences growing
more and more indistinct, he merely murmured :

" Ozone be hanged. I mean—something to rouse

Q

in us—a 'strornry feelin—of xstrorny drowsi-
nus—it's very odd : my eyes won't open keep—
think—if you'll xcuse me—I'sh go—right—off
sleep ! "

As he said, so he did. Shifting his position
to another peak which contained more grains
than the first, and provided him with a comfort-
able back to lean against, the ex-monarch smiled
seraphically but feebly upon his captain ; let his
head wag gracefully sideways to the right ; and
then with his face fixed upon the sky with
very little expression in it, he slept, and snored.
The regularity of his breathing indicated the
tranquillity of his conscience.

Binko gazed upon the slumbering lieutenant
with inarticulate rage. That he should presume
to go to sleep in his presence, and at such an
awkward crisis in the fortunes of the Blues, was
in defiance of all the rules which he had laid
down for their conduct. So he used violent
language as soon as he found his voice, which
was indeed nothing new ; and he shook Odonto

vigorously without the slightest effect. Meanwhile the airy spirits of the Reef, which had treated Odonto gently, began to buzz about the ears of the pirate-chief in a most annoying manner, to sting him in the most uncomfortable places, to run hot little pins into him which caused excruciating pain, and generally to make themselves merry at his expense. He looked about him, but could see nothing; and when he yelled at his fairy-tormentors they only tormented him the more. Meantime soft and strange sounds of music were heard in the air. The * ojnab, his own favourite instrument, suddenly resounded close to him. Tambourines were beaten without warning all round his head, and occasionally upon it. Voices without bodies whispered the rudest remarks in his ear; and fingers without voices rapped out " Binko! Binko!" upon the white rocks, and even wrote down in visible letters " Yah! Binko," under his very nose.

And now a very curious thing happened. The invisible instruments in the air began to play

a strange Chloralic tune, subsequently transferred
to other maps and countries under the title of
" We're all nodding " ; and at the different points
and passages of the Reef the various members
of the band (not the orchestra, but the crew)
were seen to stagger on to the platform where
Binko was swearing, all in more or less advanced
stages of sleepiness. Binko, still awake through
the malice of the sprites and the ferocity of his
temper, began at once to roar at them in his old
genial fashion, as if he were still upon his quarter-
deck. " Mutinous wretches," he exclaimed, " how
dare you face your injured captain ? I'll court-
naval the pack of you ! lubbers ! lobsters ! sons
of a sea-cook ! sea-Cook's tourists !—why ain't
you drowned and done for ? "

" Don't shout," murmured Indigo. " We want
to go to sleep."

" We didn't drown," pursued Verditer with a
yawn which nearly dislocated him, " because we
were born to stretch."

" What do you—confound it," cried the pirate,

as he too began suddenly to yawn, "what do you do that for? it's catching. Here, don't lie down—stand up!"

With an instinct of obedience the crew tried to obey, but instantly collapsed all along the line. Fast asleep or fast becoming so, their manly forms curled into the surrounding rocks in many attitudes, becoming or otherwise, and the genius of the Reef began to overpower them all. Binko indulged in another ineffectual roar, half-strangled in his throat by the sleep that was gaining on him. "Give it up," said one of the crew quietly. "Anger is incompatible with yawning. Good night."

"More flat mutiny!—very flat this time," exclaimed the pirate-chief as he looked at the position of his prostrate followers. "And somehow or another I can't help winking at it myself," he added, as his eyes began to refuse to keep open, all others on the Reef being now close shut. "Get up," cried he with a spasmodic revival of the temper; and so saying he kicked the nearest sleeper, who received the salute in contemptuous silence. "By Jove! won't we square accounts to-morrow morning! But as I require obedience, shut all eyes! Quite right. I say, Odonto, this won't do, I find I'm getting very sleepy too. My eyes begin to droop, my legs to stagger, ah! What can it mean? nor poppy nor mandragora, nor all the drowsy syrups of the fair and soothing Dame Vinslovia can compare (although for teething infants a specific), to . . . this . . . queer climate . . . as a . . . sopo . . . rific! As somebody said, goonigh."

And the distinguished pirate slept like a child.

CHAPTER XIII.

THE USE OF THE CORAL RING.

YES : the pirate slept. He was a beautiful object in his own way, the sun considerately drying the creases in his frock coat, and starching his limp collars with the natural heat of the latitude. I say latitude because Binko was indeed as broad as he was long, and therefore latitude was his natural element. Casual bees lighted upon that attractive nose, and lingered for a time about its pronounced contours and rich varieties of colouring. The spirit of a deep sleep brooded strangely over the whole strange scene, and the heavy hum of silence was upon the face of the world.

Two forms of a far more pleasing shape and kind
than those on which we have been recently gazing
now occupied the foreground of the picture.
Nothing can ever make so pretty a foreground
as a pair of young wedded lovers, or, for that
matter, so pretty a background either; and
Floriline and Osy, emerging from the water upon
the high and dry ground, whether fore or back,
fulfilled the conditions to perfection—the perfection
of both, but particularly of the young queen. His
manly arm clasped her delicious waist, and under
the loving protection of the fairies both appeared
absolutely dry. Not that I mean that they
wanted to drink anything, save only of each
other's eyes. And they began to exchange sweet
converse at once, in the mystic language of the
Reef.

She said—" Oh, this is bliss ; my cup is over-
flowing ! "

He said—" It is—with water."

She said—" Love, where are we going ? "

He responded—" Darling, how can I tell ? "

She replied, with a passionate enthusiasm—
"Where'er we go to, 'tis you my life this moment
that I owe to. My foot you shielded with your
best golosh; and underneath your guinea macin-
tosh, you gave your Floriline complete protection!"

"It is the water-proof of my affection," he replied.
And they sate upon a convenient rock, and hugged.

"I do not, I confess," the Baron Osy proceeded,
"look upon this as a purely delightful prospect.
It is but a barren look-out for a baron, all things
considered. The view is dreary, and it makes one's
eye ill, to gaze on rocks—rocks *et preterea nihil.*"

"Moreover," added the queen, "it feels to me
very like luncheon-time; and I was always fond
of luncheon, though the court-physician objected
to my eating any more when I was hungry than
when I wasn't. Sweet, what are we to live on?"

"Bread being the staff of life, on our own twist, I
suppose," said the Baron Osy. "At all events, it
looks as if we must live on the rock."

"What, like a crumpet?" she observed.

"Sweet angel, you mean a limpet!" said he.

"I mean on anything that sticks to the rock—
whelks, for instance. And by Jove," he proceeded,
"here is something that does. Thanks to heaven,"
as his eye fell casually upon the wondrous form of
Binko, "here at last is a native!"

"An oyster!" exclaimed Floriline. "Oh, happiness! Open him!"

Osy advanced eagerly with a blunt pocket-knife
to fulfil his queen's behest; but saw at once that
the oyster was Binko, and expressed himself
strongly accordingly. The pretty queen turned
white with fear, and shrank to her lover's side.
"It is, indeed, that horrid little man!" she said.
"And talking of crumpets, here are his raga-
muffins sleeping too! Oh, Osy-Posy! what are
we to do?"

"All as fast asleep as the Sleeping Ugly!" he
said, alluding to an ancient fairy-tale which was very
popular in Tadt. Whereat the Baron Osy began
to yawn with an infinite baronial grace. "And,
strange to say, I scarcely now can keep myself from
falling down and going off to sleep myself!"

" Osy, my own Osy, baron of my choice, don't !"
exclaimed Floriline. " Besides, it's dreadfully rude
to yawn like that ; and remember in what danger
we are, and that we're wrecked—and that—Osy,
my love and husband, don't go to sl—— why, I'm
going there myself ! What does it mean ? Oh,
my own Osy, pinch me ! You have done so ere
this in secret, and I have forgiven you ! Osy—
Os—O—zone—oh ! "

" Bye-bye ! " with difficulty ejaculated the Baron
Osy de Ankworks. And he, too, slept. It was a
very odd place to be wrecked on, certainly.

*   *   *   *   *

" There is a screw loose somewhere," murmured
the young queen, as she looked round, and felt
the influence of the place gaining possession of
her. " Binko's-crew," she added, still in unconscious obedience to the laws of her own land,
which of course queens ought to be the first to
obey. " How in the world have we got here,
and where in the world have we got ? Goodness
gracious, I know ! this must be the Chloral Reef

about which that dreadful old Shpex was always
talking. There was a lecture of his about its
volcanic motion, and the effect of the cosmic dust
blending with the soporific and opiate action of
the pumice-stone when seen at a distance through
an aqueous atmosphere, which I shall never
forget. I think it appeared in the *Nightlightly*,
and was called the Monologue of the Dratopore,
or something like that. I remember my dear Osy
being very funny about it, and saying that
Dratopore sounded like an Eastern town expressed
in bad language. But all the Sage-green Committee
declared that it was the most lucid thing Shpex
had ever written, so I pretended to understand
all about it. You can always pretend to understand Shpex, because as he doesn't know what
he means himself, he can't find out that you don't.
Anyhow I did understand the wonderful story of
the Hebetites, and how they all go to sleep here.
I remember a couple of Hebetites being exhibited
at Kashburg, and everybody running after them.
Gracious! shall I become a Hebetite? I'm going to

sleep as fast as I can. Osy, dear Osy! Euchrisma,
where are you? I want you to call me in the
morning. Where's my maid—drowned?"

"Not at all," was the immediate response of
the handmaiden. "I only swam in the back-
water, as becomes my place. Knowing you'd
certainly need my assistance, I saved myself at
a respectful distance!"

"That's right : now if your dress contains a pin,
produce the point, shake me, and run it in!
Gaze but around, you see upon the rocks sights
to expose you to electric shocks! Since man first
crossed the line, say on what shore so many sleepers
crossed the line before? There's danger in the
air, and all around, while one by one fall slumbering to the ground. Mere useless-lumber lie our
hated foes. The wind's nor'-east from Binko's shape-
less nose! While Osy, too, in dangerous proximity,
sleeps like an infant in the snowsiest dimity!
And as for me, I feel that I must try an early
closing movement for my eye! Euchrisma!"

And the maid cried, "Lawk, the queen is going

to fall! The Baron—Binko—Heavens! I see it all!"

When anybody sees it all, there is always a crisis at hand. The pretty Floriline was making desperate efforts to keep awake. She had heard wild tales of the Reef, but she did not know with any certainty what might be likely to happen. But she had heard that the first to sleep would, by the law of the place, be the first to wake, and saw herself and her husband at the mercy of the pirate. Bravely the sweet queen pinched herself black and blue, and welcomed the keen point of the pin which her obliging maid ran into her. But the mighty genius of the place was fast becoming too potent to be resisted; and overpowering sleep was relaxing all her muscles in spite of every effort she could make, when—what was it she heard? Just a voice, and no more: a sweet whisper of a voice like a sigh of the wind in a pine tree, belonging to nobody, but remembered at once as having been heard by her once before in days when she was a very little girl. Very softly and very clearly it

whispered, "Floriline, have you forgotten your
talisman? Do you remember who put the coral
ring on your finger, and when you were to use
it? When you are in real and great danger, and
cannot——"

"'And cannot keep yourself awake!'" cried
Floriline half asleep, but at once remembering.
"'And when he whom you shall love best shall
be by your side and in the same danger, turn
the coral ring twice on your finger, call steadily
three times three on the name of the fairy—the
fairy——'"

"Robur!" whispered the voice.

"'Robur, and do not be afraid.' No, I won't be
afraid," said the pretty queen. "There's Euchrisma
gone off to sleep too, and I'm alone with the dear
fairy friends who have been so constantly with me
n my dreams, and I'm not going to be afraid of
them. I'm just awake enough to do what they
tell me, and leave the consequences to them.
Robur," her soft voice appealed, "Robur, Robur!"
She turned the coral ring three times, and it

seemed magically to
enlarge itself so as
to be turned easily;
and three times at
each turn she pro-
nounced the talis-

"FEAR NOTHING, CHILD," THE SPIRIT SAID, "I AM THE TEA-SPIRIT."

manic name. At the end of the first turn a
strange green light quivered in the atmosphere,

and in the background a few pumice stones appeared to dissolve into the middle of it; at the
end of the second a deep hue of black seemed
to blend with the green, and a weird cloud of
cosmic dust to be thrown into the eyes of anybody
who might have been there to see, but wasn't; at
the end of the third a beautiful and rainbow-like
figure took form and substance out of the surrounding haze, and with clear and wakeful eyes looked
protectingly down upon the young queen's sinking
form. " Fear nothing, child," the spirit said, " I
am the Tea-spirit, the most beneficent of created
genii ; and I am here to wake you."

CHAPTER XIV.

SHPEX explained it all, afterwards, in an article of such profound learning, and words of such an extraordinary length, that the *Intellect* (as the magazine was called in which he published it), never came out any more. The subscribers broke down entirely. He showed precisely the chemical elements of the vision which appeared to Floriline, and that there was nothing supernatural about it. That nothing supernatural ever could have happened, because the moment it happened it became natural, was the line of proof upon which Shpex and his friends always proceeded.

The appearance of Robur to Floriline was, as Shpex showed, the necessary consequence of the conditions of the aerolithic nimbus.

To Floriline, however, the beautiful spirit which she saw presented no such ideas at the time. It was a dainty and graceful spirit, robed in soft tints of interwoven black and green, of which the green had the appearance of being the stronger. In the spirit's face was a kindly domestic look, as of some dear housewife watching always over the infinite purities of home; and a companionable simmering sound rose round about her, while a welcome fragrance seemed at the same time to steal into the enchanted air.

"Sweet spirit, what are you?" cried the kneeling Floriline, half hiding her face in wonder before the gracious apparition.

"Don't you know?" said the spirit. "Then listen!

> "*I arise from chest and caddy,*
> *Black-and-green-clad, as you see,*
> *Just the sweetest spirit living,*
> *Spirit of delicious tea!*

Lovely woman loves of all things
Little cups of me to mix
For her relatives and friends, be-
tween the hours of four and six:
And, though men profess to shun me,
Numbers of them you may see
At their clubs, at five, indulging
In clandestine draughts of tea.
They may talk of wine and beer, who
Drown their senses in the cup;
When you want your wits about you,
Call for me—I'll wake you up!"

The soft sounds filled the air with music, and Floriline felt the heavy hand of sleep lifting from off her eyes. Then too, the spirit with a kindly smile began gently to wave over the heads of Osy and Euchrisma the fairy wand she bore (the spirit being essentially feminine), and they too began to return to the world of consciousness. Binko and his snoring crew remained outside the circle of that magic power, though the convulsive movements of their sleeping forms, and stifled utterances, sugges-tive of strong liquors and indigestion, betrayed a decided uneasiness at the neighbourhood of an unusual object. Even the waking Osy looked upon the strange spirit with some suspicion, as he rubbed his eyes and gaped at her with the peculiarly foolish and confused expression of one just aroused from sleep. " Wannaygooshish," was his first remark, as he sat up, imagining himself in bed, and gazed. This he modified immediately afterwards into a very deliberate. " What in the name of goodness is this ?—I arise from dreams of tea, at dyspeptic hours of night," he proceeded, growing mixed. " Good-morning, thank you, what time is it ? Ah ! Who's the parti-coloured party ? "

" Osy, my darling," said the queen, " let me present you. This is the tea spirit, Robur. And this is the Baron Osy. Osy—Robur. Robur—Osy."

" You're right," remarked the baron, still sitting up frog-like on an imaginary bed. " It certainly is being presented, for I doubt if we have practically met before. I know thee not for purposes of suction : and this is, almost, our first introduction." The spirit smiled upon the young man with a smile of exquisite gentleness, and began again.

" Nay, I'm a good strong spirit, credit me :
There are no limits to the strength of tea !
Show me the place, I pray, where I am not ;
The rich man's palace and the poor man's cot,
The master's parlour and the servant's hall,
The club—the tavern—I pervade them all !
I am the old maid's lord, the bachelor's bride,
The pauper's wealth, the advertiser's pride !
My home I carry with me, not a doubt of it,
For, brought from Delph, the world still drinks me out of it !"

" 'Twas whispered in heaven, 'twas muttered somewhere else !" exclaimed Queen Floriline in despair. " Is this a time for conundrums ?"

"Don't cross your T when you want it most," whispered Osy to his beloved encouragingly. " But allow that it's very kind of it—or him or her—to prevent us from being caught napping !"

" It was very natural on her part," said the smiling spirit, who of course heard everything. " And I ought to beg pardon for talking so much. But gossip, you know, always will come with tea ! But don't be frightened ; I am here according to the great fairy law, to get the sweet god-child of the fairies out of her straits, and over them. Our mighty fairy-influence is unhurt by time, and laughs at the wisdoms and discoveries of men, shielding our favourites with an impregnable defence. My magic ship is ready for you, children, to take you back to Tadt, where things are going badly without you. As for that evil pirate and his band, let them take their meed. Let them and theirs be Hebetites for ever!" And over the young heads of Floriline, Osy, and Euchrisma, the fairy Robur waved her wand once more, while out of the water, which was now sparkling at the base of the reef like a child at play, as if there had never been such a thing as a storm in the world, there rose to view a wonderful magic vessel. It seemed but small in size; and its whole extent was occupied by the form of a huge ox standing on its four legs, and gazing at the prospect with a ruminating air. It appeared to be the whole crew and the whole cargo, and nothing else was visible.

" My !" said the fair Euchrisma.

" Gracious !" exclaimed the queen. " Are we to sail on that ? Why, there's no room !"

"There's no room for the ox," said Robur gravely and with some disapproval of Floriline's want of confidence. "If the wondrous craft can carry him, be sure it can carry you."

"But what about our feeding on board?" asked Osy.

"The animal makes every kind of soup," replied the fairy, "and also supplies tinned meats in profusion. My attendant spirits, Congou and Oopack, will be at hand with tea at all times, and the hours of the voyage will pass like minutes. Come!" And as she waved her wand again, the three felt all heaviness and sense of sleep leave them, and stepped upon the fairy vessel, which expanded gracefully to make room for them. Conveniently disposed about the deck were many tea-chests, which made benches and berths and anything else that was wanted. Floriline clapped her hands with delight as she examined every corner of the magic yacht, and the soft but unexpressive eyes of the mystical ox rested upon her as she moved.

"Ta-ta, Binko!" laughingly she called out to the

sleeping pirate. "He'll be pleasant with his crew when he wakes, and they will probably dispose of him. My dear fairy, what will become of his Blues?"

"My love," said Osy, "never mind. Wise people always leave the blues behind them, as we are going to do."

"But oh, fairy," appealed Floriline, "I should like to see the little man in a temper once more, and after all I don't want him to starve. Can't you send another fairy ship for him, and land him somewhere where he can become a betting man, I mean a better one?" A soft and favouring breeze was filling the sails of the fairy-yacht, and the music of the invisible spirits sounding in the air.

"Well," said the fairy, looking a graceful picture at the helm, "let us see what we can do with him." And she waved her wand in the direction of the spot where Binko lay. Soon his fierce little eyes began to twinkle, and he rolled first one way and then the. other, and gradually sat up. "Was it a dream," he said, "or did I have to swim?

Where is my morning glass of *mur-and-klim ?
I'm damp, so please take the chill off my tub ; the
usual game—bath, towel, and the rub. I'm un-
accustomed publicly to swear, but where the
dickens have I got to ? There ! "

"How do, Binkie ? " observed Osy with a wave
of the hand. The pirate realised the situation, and
at once turned all the colours of the rainbow. He
burst into wild execrations of everything and
everybody, and danced upon the rocks. He kicked
his Blues at random, and under the influence of the
wand which Robur waved at intervals they all
began to wake up in various attitudes of profound
stupidity. "Hi!" he said frantically, as the bark
spread her sails, " Conductor! Give us a ride !
Take me from the Bank ! Hi !"

"Full inside," answered the fairy smilingly.

"Murder !" he said. " Up, Blues, and at 'em !
I'm baffled and betrayed ! Are those two going to
escape me after all ? And must they wed for
better or for worse ? Take as my marriage gift the
pirate's curse ! May all your dearest ventures turn

to ill! May you be choked with Elkcoc's biggest pill! May Shtiffirg prove to you an unsafe man! May Rolyat's largest and unsightliest van remove whole families all day and night where'er you turn your miserable sight! May Madam Nella's hair restorer make your heads' two halves two different colours take ; the while some terrible old man of sin offer you Boban pickles with a grin! May fiery *dratsum all your dreams monopolise from every dead wall in the whole metropolise, and at your head in awful type be hurled the largest circulation in the world!" And the pirate sank back foaming at the mouth, while his Blues sat half-awake all round him hugging their knees, like a party playing at hunt-the-slipper.

"Poor man!" said Floriline compassionately, "he's growing quite confused. I'm sorry you have been so disappointed, Binko. Good-bye!"

"I say, don't leave a fellow in such a hole as this," pleaded the pirate, changing his tune and whining. "I've finished my curse, upon my soul! Take me home, away from these wicked companions of mine,

and I'll be a good man, indeed I will. I have long
secretly but sincerely loathed my evil courses."

"After all those courses you must take your
dessert," said the fairy, sternly. "Stay on that
rock ! "

"It hurts so," said Binko, piteously, as he began
to realise what he was sitting on.

"Poor fellow !" said the gentle Floriline. "After
all, his crime was love. Perhaps he'll turn over
a new leaf, if we let him."

"'Pon honour, I will," said the pirate.

"Then listen," said the fairy. "On this bark
you cannot travel; for the law of her fairy-being
forbids her to carry such very third-class passengers.
But you shall be rescued from the doom of the
Reef in the fairies' own time and way, if you will
do as I tell you."

"I'll do anything !" Binko yelled, as the fairy-
bark began to recede from the shore.

"Very well, then. Swear to give up *nig and
* mur, and stick to me."

"Who are you ?"

" The Spirit of Tea."

" —— " (Answer not recorded. It was too shocking.)

" You've got to do it ; and take the pledge."

" It won't cost anything, captain," whispered Odonto, who was now at the other's side. " You can break it when you get home. Besides, you've lived on water all your life already if it comes to that.

" Done then," said Binko.

" And you'll give up all your piracies ? " said the fairy.

" Certainly. But how am I to live ? "

" Bless you, captain," said the lieutenant, " you can go on taking people's money and lives too, in the way of honest business. Get 'em to make you the chairman of a particular kind of railway company I've heard of."

" The thought is happy," answered the pirate.

And so the matter was arranged. After a certain time for reflection and amendment, the spirit gave her fairy word that Binko and his band should be called for on the Reef; from the dangerous influences of which enchantment should meantime preserve them. And Floriline and Osy parted from their abductors upon quite friendly terms, as a delicious perfumed breeze sprang up at the fairy-vessel's stern, the deep blue waters leaped and glistened round her keel, and — the mystic ox uttering a long, musical low—the pair who had gone through so strange a trial sped away, under spirit-guardianship, towards the longed-for shores of Home.

CHAPTER XV.

THE shores of Home were in a very disturbed condition. When all that the Tadtite fleet could do, and all the telegraphs, telegrams, telephones, telescopes, teleotes, teleosms, telephuges, and tele-legs, with all their exertions could find out nothing whatever about the whereabouts of Floriline (whose absence lasted altogether for a period of ten months, eight days, fifteen hours, and one minute :—but for the magical flight of the fairy-yacht it must have been longer), it was obvious that a regency must be appointed to avoid anarchy, and everybody suddenly began to wonder who was responsible for anything, and to find out that nobody was. It was really surprising to find out how much one young girl had done to keep the machine together. Shpex argued for the claims of the Sage-green Committee to be considered the chief authority in the country; the Lord Honidhu pointed out that law was supreme over everything, and that the public spirit and unequalled disinterestedness of the Rab entitled them to an undoubted position at the head of affairs; Count Sapo de Pears dwelt upon the enormous number of paintings which were exhibited all over Tadt every year (upon walls now let out by the acre) as a proof of the rich fruitfulness of Tadtite art, and the fitness of exhibitors to govern through a self-chosen committee of forty; Lilliflop appealed to the poetic and upholstering sides of the artistic nature, as supplying the true line of beauty for an enlightened government; and Admiral Tambourini advanced the claims of religion to the sound of a full orchestra of tongs and bones, parading everywhere in the streets with much noise of converted vivandières and much disturbance of the working and the suffering; but sounding his own trumpet so 'umbly and lustily withal, and collecting so many subscribers, that even dignified prelates began to make advances to his vivandières, and the world seemed in danger of forgetting that, unlike the drama, religion has one form not to be permitted, which is called burlesque. Everybody, except those who had any gift for it, began to rush into pen and ink; and all the upper classes agreed to rule for themselves through newspapers of their own. They wrote them, sold them, and bought them, all for themselves, composing them entirely of small scandals about each other, writing each other's lives on doubtful facts supplied by themselves, and delighting the public by full accounts of what the great Nosnibor dined upon when at home. The public, who had never heard of the great Nosnibor before, were naturally anxious to avail themselves of the new education. And if this class of writers aimed at their amusement, there was another to which I have before alluded, which existed entirely

S

for their instruction, and at once began with the help of Shpex to plead the claims of Pure Culture, from which everything that could by any possibility amuse was to be excluded (which really, when you came to examine it, was about all that Pure Culture meant) to the superintendence of Tadtite education. The Culturists, too, wrote chiefly about each other in a set of small journals of their own; and though none of them had ever done anything whatever, individual, or original, or worthy of note —they mentioned each other's names so constantly and so systematically as "that eminent thinker"— "that enlightened critic"—etc., etc., that the public began to hear of their names in spite of itself, and to suppose that these gentlemen really had done something, though when they were asked what, neither the public nor the gentlemen themselves could say. So, between these two different classes of writers who wanted to divide all the writing of the day, the few people who still believed in the simple and direct virtues of the old Tadtite language, and wanted to read something neither too light nor too dark, began to wonder what was going to be the end of it. For the worst of it was that a body of men called the *Sserp, who, as a plain fact, really had a greater influence in Tadt than any other body of men, and exercised it on the whole both loyally and well, to the steady and constant advance of the interests of the country, and the welfare of the poor and oppressed, were beginning to be themselves rather confused by the growing and intense desire of everybody who was nobody to be written and talked about, and to find it difficult to distinguish between the brazen trumpet and the golden cymbal. And when at last they began to fail to distinguish between the doings of royal personages (which, however foreign, had always been respectfully chronicled) and those of the court-tragedian Monopol, and to record every day not only what he acted, but where he dined and who dined with him, and what he said after dinner in returning thanks for the toast of his health (which some eminent person was usually retained to

s 2

propose), the outside world (still not an insignificant population) began to be at first astonished, then to chuckle, and then to laugh. And when the world really begins to do that, it is generally

WHAT HE SAID AFTER DINNER IN RETURNING THANKS FOR THE TOAST OF HIS HEALTH.

the beginning of the end. But Monopol and others of the above chuckled considerably themselves, and made hay while the sun shone.

The world began to laugh rather openly, before

the absence of Queen Floriline was over, at all
the wonderful pretensions from various quarters
which we have been just describing. For, finding
it absolutely impossible to agree upon any first
magistrate, where everybody felt (or at all events,
felt bound to say) that there were no claims like
his own, at last various deputations from the
various bodies above mentioned formed themselves
into regiments, adopted the name of the Admiration Army,[1] and set up in the principal market
place of Kashburg a colossal statue of the Giant
* Gubmuh, before whom they all fell down and
worshipped after the principal officers had solemnly
winked at each other ; and instituted to his honour
and their own glory the Feast of the Buttered
Trumpets, which was intended to be annual, but
prematurely ceased out of a wearied land. The
figure was of pure and hollow brass, but, thanks
to its enormous proportions, it was immediately
let out by contract to an enterprising firm of

---

[1] This phrase was first used by the writer in the pages of
Punch.

bill-posters, who covered it all over with advertisements, so that the material had the appearance
of being after all nothing but paper.

It might of course have been supposed that whilst
the Crown was in commission, the Uncommons
would have been the persons to decide on the
course to be taken. So it was first thought that
they would : but to everybody's astonishment it
proved, when Floriline's abduction brought the
gentlemen of the Uncommons to a test, that they
broke down altogether like an india-rubber ball
when you run a pin into it. It turned out that
of late years they had talked so much and done
so little—had so entirely left all the saying to
those who had the least to say—had so forgotten
the rules of manners in the rude and personal
remarks they kept on making to each other, which
would not have been made or borne for a moment
in any other assembly of gentlemen in the world
— and nevertheless had all the time kept on
making such a fuss about their dignity (which
was in no danger in the world from any human

being but themselves—as indeed no real dignity
ever is), that when the pinch came nobody cared
two straws about them. And the worst of it was
that the whole difficulty rose out of the conduct
of a certain set of them who had no reasonable
business to be at all in the Uncommons, and
represented only themselves, but for some reason,
unintelligible to the public, could not be put down
by anybody. Of course the Uncommons held
several sittings during those trying months :
turned out a ministry and elected another at each,
no sitting lasting less than twenty-three hours,
and absolutely nothing being done at any one
of them except the perpetual calling to order of
gentlemen who declined to come to it ; and at last
somebody dissolved the House and appealed to
the country, which took the extraordinary course
of refusing to return anybody. One side was so
positive that an era of unequalled prosperity was
before Tadt, and the other so more positive that
it was hopelessly dishonoured, and going to rack
and ruin, that the Tadtite people at last believed

neither, and became so disgusted that they declared
they would manage themselves.

One strange and sinister figure stood out in
singular proportions : that of the Master of Cold-
pore. He was the first man ever known who had
used for the purposes of the now general worship
of the idol * Nommam a profession not supposed
to be so applied, the calling of the patriot, in the
nominal service of the colony which was described
in the first chapter, and he had made patriotism
pay. The colonists were simple, warm-hearted,
and lovable, making the best mothers and soldiers
and friends in the world, suffering from old-world
wrong which all Tadt was longing to cure, but
easily led and played upon. The Master was cool
and impassible, scrupulously polite (where it might
be injurious to be otherwise), and capable of assum-
ing interest without enthusiasm. He was the most
finished master of the use of the cat's-paw whom
history has seen : and when murder and outrage
followed with deadly persistency on the march of
his passionless denunciation, he had but to wash

his hands. Sometimes, after some outrage of special atrocity, he was perhaps not very visible for some days, and it was whispered that he went about armed. But personal courage was not a requisite for the paid school of patriotism. For every wretched life among the ill-starred colonists, which through some strange fatality had to be sacrificed in his cause, either at the murderous attack of some life only less wretched than the first, or by the bitter and miserable retaliation of the block, he only seemed to be followed the more—for what was that to him? He that struck no blow had nothing to fear, and the subscriptions of the grateful colonists made him a rich man for life, and set him upon his feet among the class of men who, for owning the land (as for that matter they did in Tadt too), were the especial objects of his patient tactics of attack. His career was a great success, and a greater lesson. There were weak and fanciful minds which seemed ever to see skeletons in his wake; while in their ears, as they saw him, sounded the fairies' whisper,

"Thou art the man!" Had his motives been pure as snow, his name to them was Incarnate Murder. And men did not care to make him king in Tadt.

It is not to be wondered at that things were growing very uncomfortable in Tadt generally when those ten months, eight days, fifteen hours, and one minute, came at last to an end. The vicissitudes which the country went through in that after-all-not-very-long time were simply extra-ordinary. The prayers for the restoration of the young queen were loud and universal, when suddenly on a fine morning.in early summer (so fine after a very bad season that everybody began to be hopeful, and talk about queen's weather, the moment he got up) all the telegraphs and telegrams, telephones and telescopes, teleotes and teleosms, telephuges and telelegs, announced with universal consent at all the centres of intelligence in all the principal cities, that Floriline and Osy had landed on the Cocoa-grounds safe and sound; and attended by the maid-of-honour, without whom the landing would not have been legal. The noise of the joy-bells, the excitement of the populace, and the general relief of everybody, exceeded description. The mob danced round the colossal statue of Gubmuh, and after defacing the advertisements, pulled the statue down. The firm of bill-posters brought an action against Shpex, who, in spite of an eloquent charge in his favour from the Lord Honidhu, was cast in damages almost as heavy as his last article, and, thinkers being proverbially subjective, appealed for a subscription in vain. The Admiration Army made the most of the opportunity, and met the young queen with a procession so intensely artistic and musical (headed by Monopol, who had appointed himself home-secretary for the time), that its fame will always live in the memory of the gentleman who never dies— the oldest inhabitant. The reporters outdid themselves in adjectives, and the excited mob, in entire good humour, absolutely forced a bottle of * trop down the throat of Phœbus Apollinaris. Osy and Floriline, fresh from the fairy diet of Robur (now once more returned into protecting invisibility), looked a handsomer and more winning pair than even on their marriage-day. Great was the astonishment of the pretty queen, on naturally asking for her faithful Uncommons, to be told that there were none ; still greater to hear that the quiet gentlemen in the offices were going on as usual, and that it did not make much difference. But everything that Floriline wished was law to her faithful subjects, and on her pointing out that she must have some ministers of some kind, a new election was immediately held, and the best House of Uncommons chosen which was ever known. Nobody in it ever abused anybody else ; after a division everybody shook hands, and all parties agreed that they would do their very best for Tadt upon some general principles to be determined in committee of the whole House. Nobody spoke without first passing a preliminary examination to see if he could make any ten people listen to him patiently for ten minutes ; and an entirely new era of happiness and prosperity dawned for Tadt.

The Admiration Army found that the world grew
so intensely tired of it, that at last it disbanded
itself for lack of recruits; the members who had
never really believed in themselves retiring with
fortunes, and the greater number, who had, with
none. Out of the queen's strange experience, her
character had acquired strength with no loss of
sweetness, and her knowledge of her own mind
led to the retirement of Shpex and his friends as
already foretold ; for as soon as she understood her
mind, what was the use of talking about it, and
what else could they talk about ? So our sweet
Floriline grew from perfect girlhood through perfect womanhood, into a perfect maturity, happy in
a husband's love and in the watchful friendship of
the fairies, though in bodily presence they were
seen no more after their ordained mission was done ;
and young Echoes and Hoppoes grew at their
mother's knees in health and grace and wisdom, to
carry on the traditions of the new era connected
with the Restoration, the new golden age of
simplicity and modesty.

As for Binko, he was brought home by the
fairies, repentant, after an uncomfortable but
wholesome probation on the Reef, accompanied by
Odonto and his reformed Blues. When they
appeared before Queen Floriline, humble and fearful,
they were received with such gentle and amused
kindness that they all wept, loudly, at once, and all
together. As all their money was gone, it was
at first difficult to know what to do with them,
but after a further period of discipline and probation they were found to be at once obstinately
honest, and astonishingly keen in the discovery of
a knave. , All foolish pretensions to crowns they
had entirely forgotten and resigned. So after
much consultation with her ministry and opposition, who now acted in perfect harmony and by
turns suggested measures on the alternate days of
the week, the most famous and effectual force of
detective police which the world of the other map
has ever seen, was organised upon highly-paid
principles—the first chief being a short and stout
little man, from whose comely features all traces

of anger and intemperance had disappeared, who kept especial and devoted watch day and night over the person of his beloved sovereign, with the aid of a reflective, sententious man of middle age, tall and thin, but resolutely faithful. Moreover the little man wrote his own memoirs, which ran through five hundred editions in the first month, and brought him both fame and money. And as sweet Queen Floriline wished the strange events of her reign to be kept always green in the memory of Tadt, the celebrated detective force, to the membership of which the slightest lapse from the severest virtue was fatal, was known for ever and for ever by the name of " Binko's Blues."

THE END.